ILLUSIONS OF
REALITY

ILLUSIONS OF REALITY

BRIAN SCOTT ROMESURG

www.BrianScottRomesburg.com

Contents

Copyright

Dedication

THIS BOOK IS DEDICATED TO A VERY
SPECIAL PERSON THAT NOT ONLY GAVE
ME THE COURAGE TO CHASE AFTER
DREAMS, BUT THE BELIEF THAT I WOULD
CATCH ONE! YOU WILL ALWAYS BE
CHERISHED.

1

Chapter 1

John, a confident and successful businessman, sat quietly in a leather wingback chair of his upscale hotel room, sipping a glass of whiskey. His impatience grew as he watched minute after minute tick by on the clock, causing his leg to begin twitching in nervousness as his mind began to wonder if the person he was there to meet was going to show up as planned.

John stood up, slowly slid off his tie, and strolled across the room to pour another drink. As soon as the ice cube fell into the glass, there was a gentle knock at the door.

"You're late!" John said through a one-inch opening of the door that the safety latch stopped from opening further.

"So, I'm twenty minutes late. Big deal." a woman's voice replied.

"Twenty-five minutes late." John corrected her.

"Fine. Twenty-five minutes late." the woman snidely responded. "Now, let me in!" she demanded.

"Why should I?"

"Because I have the sweetest ass in this town, and if you

ever want to see it again, you'll open this door in five seconds." the now agitated woman said.

John immediately closed the door, flipped open the safety latch, and let Erin in.

"If you were five minutes later, I would have just started without you."

"If that's the case, why am I here? If you want some privacy, I can always leave." Erin offered.

"Because you want this as much as I do!" John replied as he squeezed her breasts and forcefully kissed her.

Erin quickly grabbed John's wrists and hastily pulled away as she said, "Slow down there, big man."

"What's the problem? You've never objected to it before."

"See these things?" Erin asked as she pointed to her blouse. "They are called buttons. They need unbuttoned, not ripped off. Last time you popped every button off, and I had to walk through the hotel lobby looking like a cheap hooker."

John smirked at the image that developed in his head.

"It's not funny, John."

"It kind of is."

"No. Really, it isn't. So, unless I have a change of clothes with me, that will not happen again. Got it?"

"Okay." John reluctantly agreed. "But you have to admit, that was pretty hot."

"I'll admit that it did turn me on knowing how much you wanted me, but there are a lot of things you do that turn me on."

"Oh yeah? Like what?" John inquired as he slowly closed what little distance was between them, causing Erin to back up in response.

The wall behind Erin abruptly stopped her retreat as John placed his hands against the wall on either side of her and pressed forward until a mere inch separated their lips.

"Aren't you going to tell me?" John softly asked, even though he was fully aware of everything that did turn her on.

Erin stood there silently, unable to speak due to the pending ecstasy that was about to unfold. Then suddenly, she lurched off the wall and locked her lips against his.

John ran his hand from the small of her back up to her head, where he grabbed a fistful of her hair and sharply pulled down, snapping Erin's head back. His lips ever so lightly brushed against the tanned and tender flesh of her neck while the warmth of his breath sent shivers down her spine.

Still half-dressed but fully aroused, John picked up Erin and tossed her onto the bed. He then positioned himself between her legs and left a trail of kisses along the length of her body up to her painted lips that let out a stifled moan as she felt him enter her.

"That's it, baby!" Erin encouraged her lover as their hips thrashed wildly together. Erin's moans grew louder as John intensified the pace and put his entire body weight into every thrust, pinning her helplessly to the mattress.

"I'm going to..." Erin tried to speak, but the sensation was too overwhelming for her.

John's body stiffened as deep rhythmic grunts emanated from his throat in perfect synchrony to every twitch that erupted inside Erin.

They laid there motionless next to each other, trying to catch their breath as the sweat slowly evaporated off their seemingly flawless physiques.

After a few minutes, John rolled over and draped his arm across Erin and said, "I wish I could spend the night with you, but..."

"John, don't lie to me." Erin sternly cut him off. "This... what we have going on is just sex. You and I both know that you will do what you always do, rush back to your perfect house, doting wife, and whatever else it is that you want more than spending the night with me."

"That's not fair, Erin. You know things are complicated right now."

"It doesn't matter. I'm driving to San Diego in the morning anyway. So, I hate to burst your bubble, but I wouldn't spend the night with you even if you begged me to." Erin told John as she flung his arm off her and got out of bed.

"Don't be like that."

"Be like what, John?"

John walked up behind her and wrapped his arms around her waist, attempting to slow her rapid dressing and pending hasty departure.

Erin wrestled away from him and said, "John, it's not like we're in love. We have physical chemistry, that's all. Now get dressed before you're late getting home."

John reluctantly gave in, slipped on his clothes, and followed Erin to the elevator.

Once they reached the lobby, John made his way to the front desk to check out of the hotel. Erin grabbed his arm to turn him towards her saying, "I'm not trying to be a bitch, John. It's just that what we have is easy. Please don't complicate things by attempting to get me to develop feelings for you because we know how that will end. Okay?"

John nodded his head in agreement as she kissed him on the cheek.

Fear quickly swept over John, and the blood seemingly drained from his face as he heard a familiar voice shout out to him from across the lobby.

"John! Good to see you. It has been at least six or seven months since we last spoke."

"Fred! Margaret! It's great to see the two of you. What a surprise!" John said in his best salesman voice.

"What are you doing here?" Fred inquired.

"Oh, I had a meeting with a client that was in town for a day. What are you two doing here?" John asked, trying to make small talk to cover his nervousness about being in a hotel with a woman other than his wife.

"We just got back from vacationing in Maui, and the flight home wore us out. So, we decided to spend the night here. When I was younger, that two-hour drive home would've been easy, but I have slowed down quite a bit in my retirement years." Fred replied.

"Hi, and you are?" Margaret asked while extending her hand toward Erin.

"I'm sorry, how rude of me. Let me introduce you to my assistant Erin."

"Your assistant. I see." Margaret suspiciously said with a raised eyebrow.

"I'm afraid I am in a bit of a rush," Erin said. "It was a pleasure meeting you." She added before quickly making her way to the exit.

Once Erin was out of earshot, Margaret asked John, "So if she is your assistant, why did I see her give you a kiss?"

"Margaret, mind your own damn business!" Fred quipped.

"No, it's fine," John assured him. "She didn't kiss me. She just gave me a quick peck on the cheek out of excitement for securing a deal that we didn't think we were going to get. That is all."

"See Margaret, it was nothing," Fred said, attempting to diffuse the situation.

"Well, I find that highly unprofessional." Margaret shot back.

"You are one hundred percent correct, Margaret. I wanted to address that, but I didn't want to embarrass her in front of you both. I assure you that I will have a talk with her about professional boundaries as soon as possible." John said.

"John, it was great seeing you again, but we need to get to our room for some rest. Take care of yourself." Fred said before ushering Margaret towards the elevators with his hand on her back.

John left feeling that he covered the situation well enough and headed home. However, there was still a tiny nagging voice in his head that had him a little worried about Margaret calling his wife to report what she had seen. But his faith in Fred being able to control that nosey woman of his gave him a bit of solace with the situation.

It was eight o'clock in the evening when John finally made it home, far later than his wife expected him to be. The first thing John noticed was the living room lights that were still on. Usually, Carol would already be upstairs in the bedroom watching television in bed, and the only light left on would be in the kitchen. John figured Margaret must have called Carol to report what she witnessed at the hotel.

Knowing that telling her the same story he had told Margaret wouldn't be believable to Carol, other possible explanations flooded his head. However, all of them would be a blatant lie to her since it didn't match Margaret's version of events remotely. Without an explanation, he knew the only thing he could do was go inside with his head held high and face the accusation that was about to be thrown at him.

"Hi, John. You're home late. Did you have a rough day at the office?" Carol asked.

"No, it was just a typical day," John replied.

"I know. I heard about it." Carol said with a cold stare.

"Then why the hell did you ask?" John shot back at her being fully aware that she knew about his dirty little secret.

"You don't have the right to speak to me like that," Carol said with tears filling up her eyes. "I can't believe you did this again."

"I'm not going to put up with this crap from you, Carol. I work hard, provide you with a beautiful home, a nice car, and give you everything that you want and need. There is nothing you do without."

"I do without a faithful husband!"

"I come home to you every night!"

"You do, John. Every night, right after you screw another whore. How do you think that makes me feel? All I want is to be loved and appreciated. Yes, the house, car, everything is more than I could have dreamed of, but all I ever wanted from you is your love."

"I do love you. That's why I come home to you at the end of every day."

"If you loved me, you wouldn't cheat on me."

"It's merely sex. It doesn't mean anything."

"It means something to me. It means that you don't love me. When was the last time you made love to me?" Carol shouted at John.

"I don't know. It's not like I put it on a calendar every time we have sex."

"I don't either, but I can tell you it was four months ago."

John shook his head in disbelief, "Maybe it was. Maybe it wasn't. I know that I am tired of being accused of having an affair every time I come home late from work or having a beer with the guys. Maybe if you didn't always accuse me of it, it wouldn't happen. Have you ever thought about that, Carol?"

"It's my fault that you cheated? How dare you!"

"I am done. I'm going to bed. This conversation is over with!" John shouted as he headed upstairs.

Carol felt devastated. She didn't know what to do or say to get John to realize that what he is doing is shattering her very soul into a million pieces. All she could do was curl up in a ball on the couch and cry herself to sleep.

II

Chapter 2

It was a difficult night for Carol after discovering that her husband had once again had another affair. It was his fifth affair that she knew about within the last couple of years. However, after the tears in her eyes ran dry, she somehow managed to forgive him just as she always had and continued being the devoted housewife to John. By morning, Carol had acted as if nothing had happened at all.

"Honey, your breakfast is ready," Carol shouted up the staircase.

A few minutes later, John sat down at the kitchen table and immediately began devouring the pancakes, bacon, and fresh-squeezed orange juice that Carol had lovingly prepared. He always enjoys Carol's cooking, but her pancakes are his favorite way to start his day.

In total silence, John sat there eating and browsing through the newspaper, barely even acknowledging Carol's existence with an occasional glance.

As Carol brought him another cup of coffee, she broke the

stillness in the room by asking John, "Would you like more pancakes?"

"No, I have to watch my weight. I don't want to get fat, you know."

Carol fought back the tears that welled up inside her. She felt that his comment of not wanting to get fat was a direct insult towards her and a reminder of the excess weight that she had gained over the seventeen years that they had been together.

It wasn't a secret that John did not find Carol attractive anymore. After he had his second affair, Carol asked him why he did it again. John bluntly told her that although he loves her, he wasn't attracted to her because she was fat. It was hard for her to hear that, but the truth was that Carol herself was disgusted with how she had let herself go. Unfortunately, every time Carol tried to lose weight, another affair of John's would come to light, making her depressed, which caused her to eat more and gain more weight. It was a vicious cycle that Carol had no idea how to break.

"I better get going," John said as he slipped on his coat. "I should be home around six."

"Okay. I'll have dinner ready for you when you get home."

Carol approached John as he opened the door to kiss him goodbye, but as she leaned in, John turned his head and offered his cheek to her.

Another crack formed in her battered heart. Her psyche just a few tiny fractures away from shattering entirely. All Carol wants is to be loved by her man the way he once had.

Carol found the strength to maintain her composure long

enough to give him a peck on the cheek and say, "Have a good day, honey."

When John left, Carol ran to the bathroom and cried yet again. She stared with hateful nauseousness at the woman in the mirror that had smeared mascara encompassing red, puffy eyes and tears running down her cheeks as she quietly admonished herself. "It's no wonder why John doesn't desire you. Look at yourself! You are hideous!" She continued to criticize her reflection for every physical flaw she could find.

In actuality, Carol was a beautiful woman. Sure, she carried some excess weight, but the only reason she feels the way she does is because of what John had said and done over the years. After all, John once did think she was the most beautiful woman he had ever seen. It was one of the many reasons why he married her.

When the tears finally ran out, Carol washed the makeup off her face before heading to the closet to retrieve the vacuum cleaner. She figured since she couldn't make herself desirable to her husband, she could at least make her house beautiful and hope that it would be enough for John to want to come home regardless of what he is doing and with whom.

Before she even got started, her cleaning was interrupted by her cellphone ringing. It was her close friend Lisa.

Carol took in a deep breath and let it out slowly, attempting to calm herself. She didn't want Lisa to know that she had been shedding tears over John's behavior yet again.

In the most upbeat tone she could muster, Carol said, "Hi, Lisa. How are you?" as she answered the phone.

"I'm doing well. I just thought I would check in with you and make sure everything is okay."

"I'm fine. Why wouldn't I be?" Carol asked.

"It's just unusual for you to miss the book club meeting we had last night." Lisa explained, "In all the years that I have known you, it has only happened a few times before that I can recall."

Lisa knew Carol well, almost too well, and it must have been evident to Lisa that John was up to his old antics again when Carol missed the meeting. After every affair he had, Carol went into a short period of reclusion from her friend, probably out of embarrassment if for no other reason.

Abruptly the conversation turned to silence as Carol didn't know how to respond. She didn't want to lie to Lisa, but she was too embarrassed to admit the truth.

"Are you still there?" Lisa asked.

"Yeah," Carol managed to squeak out.

Lisa could hear Carol's staggered breathing on the phone and said, "Oh, hon... he didn't."

"It was just a one-time thing. John isn't going to see her again. He promised me."

"Just a one-time thing like the several before, huh?" Lisa asked. "When are you going to say you've had enough and leave him? You deserve to be treated better than that."

"I love him! Besides, it's not like he's abusive and hits me or anything." Carol defended John.

"He is mentally and emotionally abusing you. The only difference between what he does and physically hitting you is that what he is doing doesn't leave bruises and scars that people can see."

"John is a good man, a great provider, and deep down in

his heart, I know he loves me too. It isn't anything that I can't handle." Carol again defended her husband.

"You shouldn't have to handle something like that. If John genuinely loved you, he wouldn't be cheating on you."

Carol became more and more emotional as Lisa kept pointing out the painfully obvious. It was much easier to live in a state of denial than to face the truth, and Carol had become quite adept at denying John's blatant disrespect for her and their marriage.

"I can't do this right now. I have to go." Carol said as she hung up the phone without even a goodbye.

Being emotionally drained, the last thing Carol wanted to do was relive every affair she knows John has had. To her, it was not conducive to healing the wounds that she had nursed for so long. She figured the best thing to do was focus on the present and hope for the future. But above all, leave the past in the past. Even though the past in question happened just twelve short hours ago. So, Carol turned on the vacuum and immersed herself in the task at hand, cleaning her already immaculately kept home.

It only took a couple of hours to clean every nook and cranny in the house. However, she had been through this enough times that she knew better than to sit idly because that is when her mind would begin to wander and think about things she did not necessarily want to envision. Therefore, Carol started to prepare John's favorite dinner, roasted duck with plum sauce. It was her way to continue her quest to earn John's love and devotion, as well as a time-consuming way to keep her mind occupied.

John probably only stayed with Carol for her impeccable

housekeeping and culinary craftsmanship. For Carol, although John's compassion and affection eluded her every attempt to regain it, she hoped that doing these things for him would buy her enough time to lose the weight that repulsed him.

Cooking dinner from scratch, including side dishes and dessert, occupied the rest of her day. With only about an hour remaining before the time John said he would be home, Carol put the finishing touches on the meal and elaborately set the dining room table for a romantic dinner for two, complete with candles, wine, and flowers. She wanted John to know that she still loved him immensely, regardless of their marriage issues.

A long-forgotten smile started to appear on her face, and there was an extra spring in her step as she started getting excited about John's arrival. Carol couldn't wait to share the romantic evening she had planned.

It was then that Carol's phone rang again. She hoped it wasn't Lisa. Carol didn't want this good mood of hers ruined, so she was pleasantly surprised to see it was John calling her.

"Hi, honey. Are you on your way home? I have your favorite dinner ready for you." Carol said.

"That's why I'm calling. I'm going to grab a beer with the guys from work. I just wanted to let you know. I didn't want you to think anything suspicious was going on with me getting home a little later than expected.

"Thank you, that's very considerate. I'll keep dinner warm, and we can eat when you get home. How long do you think you will be?" Carol asked.

"Probably about an hour. We're just having a quick drink."

"Have a good time. I'll see you when you get home."

Carol turned the heat down on the oven to extend the cooking time a bit, poured herself a glass of wine, and patiently waited for John. She tried to stay optimistic about the evening. After all, he was only going to be an hour late. However, as the minutes ticked by, she began to doubt what John said he was doing and with whom. Carol hated thinking those negative thoughts, but considering the circumstances, it was only natural to question things.

After an hour had passed, there was still no sign of John. With the second hour fast approaching, dinner was now officially overcooked. Carol finished the entire bottle of wine as the joyful thoughts of spending a romantic night with her husband quickly subsided, replaced by the hurt and disappointment that was all too familiar.

Carol did her best to salvage what she could of the dinner and prepared a plate for John that she put in the refrigerator with a note that read, *I'm sorry. I tried to wait for you, but I was exhausted and went to bed. I hope you had a good time. Enjoy your dinner. Love, Carol.*

Despite Carol being left brokenhearted at home, John was having a great time with his buddies at Sporty's, a local sports bar with a fantastic collection of sports memorabilia. However, the main attractions are the waitresses that wear various tight-fitting team uniforms designed to emphasize their best assets.

Surrounded by a bevy of beautiful women, it was relatively easy for John to push aside his wife for the evening. As soon as John walked into the bar, there was one woman that immediately caught his eye.

"Hey, Mike. Check out the one wearing the Detroit Tigers uniform." John said to his friend.

"Yeah, she has a great ass." Mike acknowledged.

Another guy in the group, Tony, overheard part of the conversation and asked, "Who are you two talking about?"

"Detroit," Mike replied.

"She looks great, but don't they all? I'd take any one of them home!" Tony said.

"Of course, you would. You're short, fat, bald, and desperate. You'd take anything offered to you." Peter chimed in.

"Let's grab a table in her section," John suggested as he pointed out an open table.

Within a few minutes, their server came over to their table and said, "Welcome to Sporty's. My name is Jen. What are you boys drinking tonight?"

John looked up, anticipating the object of his desire but instead saw an attractive brunette wearing a Mets uniform standing before him.

"Oh... Hi, Jen. We thought this was her section." John said while pointing to the blonde in the Tigers uniform.

"Not a Mets fan, huh?"

"I'm certainly not a Mets fan, but that's not why. We just wanted to sit in her section." John explained.

"I get it. These aren't big enough for you." Jen said while cupping her breasts with her hands and jiggling them.

"I didn't mean that either." John attempted to clarify.

"It's fine." Jen said, "Hey, Kayla, you have some fans over here."

"Okay. I'll be there in a sec." Kayla shouted back as she carried some beers to another table.

"What's the big deal which waitress is ours?" Peter asked John.

"He has a thing for the Detroit girl." Mike quickly answered for John.

"Dang, John. You have a great woman at home." Peter said, "Don't you think that you're tiptoeing the line by wanting to visit with and drool over another woman."

"Tiptoeing the line? Ha! He's crossed the line, hopped the fence, and went down the street." Mike informed Peter.

"That's enough, Mike." John said with a scowl on his face, "Look, Peter. When you climb into bed with the same side of beef every night, it's nice to have a leaner cut of meat now and then."

At that time, John's preferred server came over to the table and said, "Hi guys. I hope I'm not interrupting your conversation. My name is Kayla. Are you all Tigers fans?"

"Not at all. Peter is more into football, Tony has the unfortunate luck of being a Cubs fan, and Mike and I root for the Dodgers." John explained.

"Me too! I love the Dodgers." Kayla said.

"Then why are you wearing a Tigers uniform? Don't they let you pick the team you want?" John inquired.

"They do, but only one girl can wear each team's uniform at a time. That way, there won't be ten servers wearing a Dodgers uniform and nobody wearing the Cubs. No offense, Tony."

"No problem. I'm used to that." Tony admitted.

"So, until Tonya quits, I'm stuck with Detroit. Anyways, do you guys know what you would like?"

"The three of us," Tony said while pointing to Mike and

Peter, "will have a Michelob, and John would like your phone number."

John was not the type to embarrass easily, but his cheeks slightly turned red due to Tony's bluntness.

"So that is what Jen meant when she said I had some fans at this table. Okay, three Michelob's and one I'll have to think about it." Kayla said.

"Ignore him. I'll have a Budweiser." John said, trying not to look too eager.

"You don't want my number then?"

"No, I'd like that too. It's just that..."

"I wish you'd make up your mind. First, you tell me to ignore your friend, and now you're saying that you want my phone number. I suppose I'll grab your beers, and you can think about it." Kayla said playfully.

As Kayla walked away, John intensely studied her captivating form. He was mesmerized by her sculpted buttocks that were on complete display in the polyester baseball pants that stretched tautly around them and how, at five feet two inches tall, her petite frame further accentuated her voluptuous breasts.

"That wasn't your smoothest effort," Mike said, but it fell on deaf ears as John continued to watch and fantasize about Kayla.

"I don't think he's listening to you," Tony said.

"Hey!" Mike shouted as he swatted John's arm.

"What?"

"What the hell is wrong with you? You're acting like a damn school kid." Mike said.

"She's... I don't know. I mean, damn!" John replied., stumbling for the words to describe Kayla without ever taking his eyes off her.

Kayla quickly returned to the table with their beers and said, "Here you go, guys. Let me know if there's anything else I can get you."

"I'm still waiting for your phone number," John told Kayla.

"Oh, I wasn't sure if you genuinely wanted it. I'll see what I can do about that." Kayla said as she rushed off to another table.

"I don't think that's a good idea," Peter told John.

"You don't understand, Peter. It is easy for you to preach morals. You have a hot wife at home."

"Yes, I do. But Lauren doesn't do half of the things that Carol does for you. Hell, she can't even make toast without burning it."

"Let me put it this way to you, Peter. Do you go out to eat?"

"Yeah, I'd probably starve to death if I didn't."

"Then you are cheating on Lauren with food."

"He has a point," Tony interjected.

"No, he doesn't. That is entirely different. You don't even have a clue what you are talking about, Tony. You're not even married."

"Is it, Peter? Is it that different? Because I am starving, it's just not food that I'm starving for." John explained.

Once the liquor started flowing, the conversation switched from women and cheating to more lighthearted topics of discussion. The guys were joking around and having a blast. However, John still watched every move that Kayla made.

Kayla was well aware of John's eyes being fixated on her. So, as she made her way from table to table, she put a little extra wiggle in her walk and tossed John a few coy smiles to tempt him further.

After a few rounds of drinks, Peter noticed the time and said, "I'm going to head home. I told Lauren I would be home by seven, and I'm already late. I'll see you guys tomorrow."

"I'm not going anywhere until I get her number," John said, referring to Kayla.

"Well, what are you waiting for? Try to get it. I bet you twenty dollars that she will shoot you down." Tony stated.

"I'll take that bet! Gentlemen, I am going to show you how to hit in the big league." John said as he slipped off his wedding ring and put it in his pocket.

"You're a dog," Peter said in a tone of disgust.

As John slid his chair away from the table, he replied, "Woof, woof."

That comment sent Tony and Mike into a frenzy of barks and howls as John stood up and headed towards the bar where Kayla was standing.

Everybody in Sporty's, including Kayla, had their attention drawn to the guys at the table. She noticed John making his way towards her, and with the confidence of an all-star pitcher, Kayla stared John down as she leaned back against the bar and waited for him to step up to the plate.

A multitude of pickup lines ran through John's mind as he closed in on Kayla. Some were better than others, but it had to be a perfect one for a woman of such a caliber as Kayla. Yet, once he stood in front of her and looked into her steel blue eyes, his mind went blank.

"Do you need something?" Kayla asked, throwing out the first pitch.

"The guys and I are getting ready to leave, and..."

"Okay, I'll get your check," Kayla replied, cutting John off in mid-sentence.

"That would be great, but I was wondering if you're free Saturday. I have season tickets to the Dodgers and would love to have you accompany me to the game. They're great seats!"

"I don't know. I usually don't go out with customers." Kayla told John.

"It's just a ballgame. I'm not asking to sleep with you. Come on. We'll have a fun time."

"I'll answer your question if you answer mine," Kayla told John.

"That's fair enough. What's your question?"

"Why did you take off your wedding ring?" Kayla asked.

"You noticed that, huh?" John said in a hushed tone.

"So? Why did you?"

"Well, she passed away last year, and..."

"Strike one!" Kayla said.

"Okay. We just recently separated, and..."

"Strike two! One more, you're out."

"Fine! It's because I find you fascinating and figured you wouldn't go to the game with me if you knew I was married." John admitted.

"Married I can handle. But lying to me will get you thrown out of the game! Understand?"

"Understood. So, would you like to join me Saturday?"

"I'll have to see what the work schedule is when it comes out. Give me your number, and I'll call you." Kayla replied.

"It's probably easier if I call you."

"That's right. I suppose it would be with your wife and all." Kayla said as she quickly scribbled her number on a napkin, "Call me on Friday around noon. I should know by then if I'm working Saturday. By the way, here's your check, and tips are appreciated." She said with a smile.

Upon returning to the table, John said, "And that's the way it's done. Pay up, Tony." Acting as if he was a smooth-talking, silver-tongued devil and playing off the fact that he was utterly humbled in the presence of Kayla.

Everyone chipped in to cover their part of the bill and left a very generous tip for Kayla before heading outside. Peter was highly disheartened by John's behavior at the bar and immediately went home. Tony was soon to follow. However, Mike and John hung out in the parking lot for a while longer talking.

"Congrats on reeling in that one. To tell you the truth, I didn't think you had a chance." Mike told John.

"Are you kidding me? I can get any woman I want. You should know that by now. When have I ever failed?"

"I admit you do pretty well for yourself, but I think Peter is right. You have to start acting like the married man you are and stop all the games with other women."

"Come on, Mike! Not you too!"

"I'm just saying that Carol treats you like a king. It would be best if you showed her some appreciation for that. I could look the other way the first time or two, but I think you've had enough fun, don't you?"

"I do show her appreciation. She has a lovely home, a new

car, and all of the bills are paid. Everything she wants, she has."

"John," Mike said while shaking his head, "Never mind." Mike conceded, knowing he wasn't going to win this argument. "I better get going too. I'll see you at work tomorrow."

III

⚛

Chapter 3

It was about nine o'clock by the time John made it home from the bar. The house was completely dark and eerily quiet. Carol had long gone to bed, shutting off every light in the house. Usually, she would leave a light or two on for John, but subconsciously Carol probably didn't anticipate John coming home that evening.

Famished, John made his way into the kitchen to raid the refrigerator. Upon opening the refrigerator door, he instantly found the plate Carol had prepared for him earlier in the evening. Without reading the note attached, John ripped the foil off, crumpled it in a ball, and reheated his dinner in the microwave.

While John waited for his dinner to heat up, he sat down in his recliner, found a late-night comedy show on television, and retrieved the napkin with Kayla's phone number on it from his pocket. He sat there silently gazing at the napkin as if it was a trophy. A symbol of his manhood not lost to time, although John was a man in his late forties with graying hair.

He reminisced about Kayla's playful smile, the cute little wiggle in her walk, and of course, her knockout body, but his thoughts were interrupted by the annoying beep of the microwave informing him that his dinner was ready.

John stuffed the napkin deep in the back of his wallet, far from his wife's potentially prying eyes. Carol had never rummaged through his stuff, but John didn't need the added drama if Carol were to start feeling suspicious and did go to lengths that she had not done before to catch him.

After retrieving his meal, John began shoveling the food, one heaping forkful after another, into his salivating mouth to satisfy his hunger. Carol had spent half of the day preparing the meal that took John less than five minutes to polish off.

It didn't take long, with a stomach full of food, before John found himself constantly yawning and with a massive desire for bed. So, after the show he was watching finished, he headed towards the bedroom to retire for the night. Each step John took down the hall towards the bedroom made him grimace. A scowl grew deeper on his face as the decibels of Carol's snoring rose as he got closer to the closed door.

Standing at the bedroom door, John paused and took an exceedingly long, slow, and deep breath, trying to calm his ire before opening it. He could turn around and sleep on the couch, but this was his bed, he thought to himself. I bought it. Why should I spend an uncomfortable night on a lumpy sofa that I can't even stretch out on just because of the fat crushing my wife, making it difficult for her to breathe? John continued rationalizing his decision in his head of why he should sleep in the bed.

When John finally had the composure to open the door, he walked over to Carol's side of the bed and stared at his slumbering wife. The rhythmic rumble of a diesel engine emanating from Carol's throat was only momentarily interrupted by brief periods of silence brought on by her sleep apnea as John stood there relishing the tiny bits of silence.

Thoughts began to fill John's head as he continued to watch his wife sleep. He hated the weight she carried on her. It was the primary source of their marital issues. Not only did it make John not desire her as he once did, but it also made Carol depressed and moody at times. She was once so vibrant and full of life. That was another thing that attracted John to her as much as her once slim physique did. Not to mention the fact that she didn't snore half as loud back then.

If only she resembled Kayla more, he would have the perfect wife, John admitted to himself. But the hands of time had not been kind to Carol. Then the thought occurred that maybe Peter and Mike were right regarding their displeasure with his extramarital affairs that he was having. However, that thought exited John's head as quickly as it had popped in when Carol snorted and began to snore again.

Finally, John climbed into his side of the bed and laid down on its edge, making sure not to touch Carol. He knew if he did, Carol would roll over to snuggle up against him and snore in his ear all night, and John was so tired that he desperately needed to get his rest. As he laid there, visions of Kayla flooded his mind as he drifted off to sleep, ensuring a restful snooze and maybe even an erotic dream or two.

When morning arrived, John woke to the alarm clock's blaring chime in his usually empty bed. Carol had always been an early riser and was already downstairs preparing breakfast for him. The aroma of fresh-brewed coffee began to waft up the stairs, motivating him to get out of bed and into the shower to start his day.

Thirty minutes later, Carol's usual beckoning for John to come downstairs for breakfast echoed up the stairs. Immediately, John came down and was greeted with another hearty breakfast.

"You look nice today," Carol said.

"Thanks!"

"You smell good too." She noted, "Any special reason?" Carol asked, wondering why John went to such great lengths to look so dapper.

"Nope, just felt like looking my best today."

Carol knew right away that John must have been intrigued by another woman last night. That is the only time John pays such close attention to his grooming. However, just because he found someone he was interested in did not necessarily mean that it would lead him to have another affair. John naturally found enjoyment in knowing he was still attractive to the opposite sex like anyone else would, so Carol shrugged it off for the time being.

"How was the dinner I made for you last night?" She asked.

"It was okay. The duck was a little dry and tough, don't you think?"

"I'm sorry, honey. I tried to keep it warm for you too long."

"Yeah, I'm sorry. That was my fault. Time got away from us last night."

"Did you have a good time with the guys?"

"I did."

"That's nice. You work hard and need to enjoy yourself." Carol said, being the supportive wife that she is. "More coffee?"

"No, thanks. I'm going to work a little early today. How about I make last night up to you and take you out to dinner tonight?" John asked while putting on his jacket.

It isn't often that John wants to spend time with Carol, especially in public, so she enthusiastically answered, "I'd love that!"

"I'll be home by five at the latest," John said as Carol walked with him to the door.

"Okay. Have a good day." Carol told him while refraining from leaning in for a kiss as he opened the door. She didn't want to ruin her happiness by being rejected for a kiss, nor did she want John to feel pressured for intimacy and have him second guess his decision to take her out later in the evening. To Carol's surprise, John wrapped one arm around her shoulders and gave her a hug and a kiss on the forehead. Sure, it was a lackluster effort on John's part, but to an affection-starved woman like Carol, it meant the world to her.

As soon as John closed the door behind him, Carol rushed to her phone to call Lisa. She was so excited about John's recent attempt at what Carol figured was a reconciliation that she had to share this breakthrough with someone and who better than her closest friend and biggest skeptic of John.

"Hi, Carol."

"Lisa, you will never guess what just happened," Carol said in a euphoric tone.

"This sounds good. I haven't heard you this happy in quite some time. What happened?"

"Well, last night I cooked a romantic dinner for John, but he went out with some guys from work and came home too late to enjoy it with me. This morning he apologized, and he is taking me out to dinner tonight to make up for it. He hasn't taken me out in months. I'm so excited!"

"That's nice. I hope you have a great time."

"That's not all. When John left for work, he gave me a hug and a kiss!"

"Really?" Lisa asked in shock.

"He most certainly did. See, I told you he still loves me. He's finally coming back around and is going to try with me to make our marriage work."

"I hope you're right," Lisa said.

"Why wouldn't I be right?"

"Maybe he did something last night that he shouldn't have and is feeling a little guilty about it. Don't get me wrong. I want you to be happy. I truly do hope that you're right. I just don't want you to get your hopes up and have him break your heart again. You've been through so much as it is." Lisa explained.

"John has never felt guilty about an affair that he has had. I doubt that's the reason now. I genuinely believe that his eyes have been opened to the situation and that he wants to make things right."

"That could be," Lisa said, trying to be supportive of her friend. "You'll have to tell me all about it tomorrow."

"I definitely will. I better get off the phone. There is so much to do. I need to finish the laundry, wash dishes, make the bed, weed the garden, take a shower, do my hair and makeup, and pick out the perfect outfit for John. There has to be something in my closet that I can wear that will hide some of this fat and at least make me appear a little thinner."

"Hon, you're beautiful just the way you are."

"Thanks, Lisa. But it isn't a secret that I need to lose some weight."

"Who doesn't these days?"

"I know, but I need to lose more than most people. Plus, it would be great to have John desire me like he used to."

"John should desire you for who you are and all the things you do for him, not purely for the size of the clothes you wear, how many wrinkles you may or may not have, or any other superficial reason."

"Unfortunately, that isn't the kind of world we live in. Besides, if John is going to put forth the effort to work on his behavior, then I can put in the same effort towards losing some weight." Carol replied. "I do need to get started on the chores. I'll call you tomorrow morning, okay?"

"Okay. Have a great evening. Bye."

While Carol was checking off items on her to-do list, John made good progress shrinking the stack of paperwork on his desk at work. It looked like he was going to finish a little earlier than expected. Around noon, John was looking forward to a leisurely lunch with his friend Mike at the sandwich shop around the corner from their office.

"Hey, buddy!" John said, entering Mike's office.

"Hey, how's your day going?" Mike grumbled.

"Things are going pretty well. It looks like I'll be finished on time today for a change. How's it going for you?"

"Could be better. Nothing seems to be going smoothly for me today." Mike admitted. "I think I'm going to work through lunch and call it an early day. I'll probably take off around two or three. Do you want to grab a beer when you get finished?"

"I can't do it today. I told Carol I would take her out to dinner tonight."

"I take it that she was pretty peeved at you for getting home as late as you did last night, huh?"

"Not at all. I just felt bad about it."

"So, everything Peter told you about how you should treat Carol better finally sank in? Hey, if you're not going to go out with Kayla, would you mind if I asked her out?" Mike inquired.

"What? Are you kidding me? Hell no! I'm taking Carol out to dinner because she put in a lot of effort to cook a special meal for me, and I didn't get home early enough to enjoy it." John explained.

"That is what you feel bad about, dinner? Not because you're cheating on Carol?"

"Come on, Mike. I don't need you to start preaching morals to me. It's bad enough that I have to listen to it from Peter."

"Okay. Sorry, John."

"It's alright. I think I'm going to head back to my office and finish things up. I'll talk to you tomorrow."

Mike could tell John was slightly irked but wasn't overly concerned about his abrupt departure. He figured John would be over it by tomorrow, and everything would be back to normal between them. After all, they were best friends and have had much worse disputes in the past. Mike hoped that John got upset with the conversation's direction because he realizes what he is doing is wrong. Although Mike didn't want to anger John and jeopardize their friendship, he certainly did not condone John's behavior.

When John returned to the solidarity of his office, his thoughts quickly turned towards Kayla. He was doing so well keeping her in the back of his mind so he could concentrate on work but, since Mike mentioned her, now he can't get her out of his mind. How her flirtatious smile melts his heart, her playful banter that cheers his spirit, the swaying of her hips that stirs his deepest lustful desires, and that sweet innocent face of hers that he is convinced was just a disguise that hides the wild devil that resides within.

Although John could daydream about Kayla tirelessly for the entire day, he knew he had to focus on work for there to be a chance of keeping the dinner plans he made with Carol. If he had to cancel dinner, it would raise suspicions in Carol's mind before he even had a chance to take Kayla out. So, John quickly grabbed the next file from the stack on his desk and worked through the rest of his lunch hour.

By two o'clock, John found himself sitting at his now tidy desk that signaled the completion of his day. He contemplated what he should do with the remaining time he had before heading home. John surely didn't want to get home this early because Carol would talk his ear off. He was going to have to listen to her during dinner, which would be painful enough. John decided to go out for a drink after all, but not with Mike. He wanted to stop by Sporty's to see Kayla if he were lucky enough for her to be working, and Mike would be a downer since he has already voiced his disapproval of the situation.

About twenty minutes later, John arrived at his new favorite bar. The place was virtually empty. Only half of the televisions were on, and there were only a few waitresses huddled in a group at the corner of the bar. None of whom were Kayla.

Knowing his options were to either have that drink without the object of his desire to ogle at or go home to his wife, the choice was clear to him, and he took a seat at the bar.

"What can I get you?" the bartender asked.

"Scotch on the rocks."

"Rough day?" the bartender asked as he poured the drink.

"Nothing out of the ordinary. Just a typical day, I suppose. You wouldn't happen to know if Kayla is working today, would you?"

"Yeah. She's in the back. Want me to get her for you?"

"That would be great!" John said as his eyes instantly perked up.

The bartender pushed open the swinging door to the kitchen and yelled, "Kayla, somebody is looking for you."

"Okay. Give me a minute." A sexy young voice shouted back. John could tell it was indeed Kayla. Her voice is permanently etched into his mind to the point that he could recognize it in a crowded room full of shouting people.

Fifteen minutes passed by, but Kayla still had not come out of the kitchen. John was undeterred and continued sipping his scotch just for the opportunity to lay his eyes on her.

"Do you want another one?" asked the bartender as he pointed to John's now empty glass.

"Sure, why not."

John swung around on the barstool towards a television at the end of the bar recapping the day's sports scores. Unfortunately, because of the time of day it was, the scores were mostly for tennis and soccer, but it was better than staring at the liquor bottles lining the wall behind the bar.

When Kayla finally emerged from the kitchen, the bartender pointed in John's direction to indicate to Kayla who was looking for her. She was pleasantly surprised to see that it was John.

Kayla quietly strolled up behind John and whispered in his ear, "I hear there is an incredibly sexy man looking for me."

John spun around on the barstool with a massive smile on his face. "There you are!"

"Sorry to keep you waiting. We're shorthanded in the kitchen today, so I'm helping to get things ready for the dinner crowd."

"Wow. You can cook too?" John asked.

"Darling, I can do a lot of things that would blow your mind."

"Really? Like what?" John asked, intrigued by her statement.

"I'm sure you'll find out soon enough." Kayla replied, "What brings you in on a Tuesday afternoon?"

"I finished up work early and was thinking about you."

"That's so sweet. I get off work at four if you want to have a drink with me."

"Sure. That sounds fantastic!" John quickly responded without trying to hide his enthusiasm.

"Great. I better get back in the kitchen, but we'll talk more in a bit." Kayla told him.

As time passed, more people began funneling into the bar, so John grabbed a seat in a booth where Kayla and he could talk more openly and with fewer distractions. He sat there alone, watching the bar slowly come to life as he waited for Kayla. The situation was unfamiliar to John. He was the type of guy that got things when he wanted it and had extraordinarily little tolerance for people that made him wait. However, Kayla was different. John felt he would travel to the Earth's ends for this woman, but he could not put his finger on why.

The next hour passed by surprisingly quickly, and before John knew it, Kayla came back over to the booth and said, "I have to change out of my work clothes. I'll be back in a minute, okay?"

"No problem. I'll be here." John said as he glanced at his watch to make a note of the time.

Changing her clothes and touching up her hair and makeup took Kayla another twenty minutes before she finally came out of the locker room. To John, it was well worth the wait because she looked radiant.

"You look incredible!" John told Kayla.

"Thanks," Kayla said with a smile. "So, you know what I do for a living, what is it that you do?"

"I'm the chief marketing officer for a technology company."

"I have no idea what that means," Kayla admitted.

"I convince people to buy things they don't necessarily need," John explained.

"Oh, kind of like those late-night infomercials."

"Sort of, but for Fortune 500 companies."

"You make a pretty good living," Kayla said as a part statement and part question.

"I do okay for myself," John replied.

"Where do you live?"

"Hermosa Beach. What about you?"

"You do better than okay for yourself then. I live in Pasadena."

One of the other waitresses came over and asked, "Can I get you guys a drink?"

"I'll take another scotch," John said as he rattled the ice in his empty glass.

"Do you want the usual, Kayla?" the waitress asked.

"Yep."

"Aren't you going to introduce me to your friend, Kayla?" the waitress asked before leaving to get their drinks.

"This is John. John, this is Cassie."

"It's a pleasure to meet you," John said while extending out his hand.

"Oh, this is the hot guy you kept going on about yesterday," Cassie said.

"Oh my God, Cassie!" Kayla exclaimed while blushing. "Just get our drinks."

As Cassie walked away, John said, "Hot, huh?"

"How long have you been married?" Kayla asked.

"Do we have to talk about that?"

"You don't bring up what Cassie said. I won't bring up your wife. Deal?"

"Deal."

"Now, let's change the subject." Kayla requested.

"Hot...hmm," John mumbled under his breath.

"Married...hmm," Kayla mimicked John.

"Here you go. One scotch on the rocks and one whiskey

with a beer back." Cassie said while placing the drinks on the table.

Cassie must have lingered a little too long at the table studying John's overall appearance because Kayla cleared her throat and said with a scowl, "That will be all."

"Sorry," Cassie said as she rushed off to the bar where a couple of other waitresses were. It was apparent that she was telling them about John because she kept staring and giggling in his direction.

However, that high school behavior didn't interfere with John and Kayla continuing their conversation and getting to know one another. That one drink they were going to have together quickly became three before John realized that it was a little past five o'clock.

"Crap! I have to get going." John exclaimed.

"Hot date with the wife?" Kayla asked in a jokingly manner.

"I wouldn't say that, but I do have plans. I should've been home by now."

"I understand. I had a nice time." Kayla told John.

"Does it look like we are still on for the game Saturday?"

"I'll know tomorrow, but it shouldn't be a problem. Call me around noon."

"Alright, I'll do that." John said as he placed some money on the table, "That should cover the tab. Tell Cassie she can keep the change. Have a good night."

"You too," Kayla said with a wink.

After John left, Cassie and the other waitresses came over to the table and bombarded Kayla with questions about him.

"Where did he rush of too? He sure left in a hurry." Sheila asked.

"He had plans," Kayla replied.

"Probably with his wife," Cassie interjected.

Kayla rolled her eyes and let out a sigh.

"He's not married, is he?" Shelly asked Kayla.

"I don't think it's any of your business," Kayla said to all of them.

"Of course he is. I saw the wedding ring on his hand." Cassie said, "But, he is pretty damn sexy. I'd take him home anyway."

"You need to keep your legs shut around him. That is my man! While you are at it, keep your mouth shut too. I don't need you embarrassing me like that again." Kayla instructed her.

"Dang, Kayla. What got into you?" Cassie asked.

"I like this guy a lot. He is sweet, handsome, and rich. I don't want any of you messing it up for me."

"Sounds like you hit the trifecta with this one," Sheila told Kayla.

"I think I possibly have. So, if I am a little short with you all, especially you, Cassie, I hope you understand."

"It's okay. I suppose I would feel the same way if I were in your shoes." Cassie replied.

"Thanks, girl," Kayla said as she offered her friend a hug.

"But, if he has a brother, you'll let me know, won't you?"

"Yes, Cassie. You will be the first to know. I'm going home. I've been here long enough. You girls have a good night."

IV

Chapter 4

John knew Carol would be wary of his late arrival home, so he decided to take a preemptive measure to cover his tardiness. John stopped at the local florist and purchased her a beautiful bouquet. It was something that he had not done for her in years. But, if John was going to play the game, he had to play it right and act like a committed and loving husband. Any indication of being less than faithful would either cost him his marriage or his new love interest, both of which John did not want to lose.

With flowers in hand and an elaborate cover story concocted in his head about why he was late, John walked through the door and shouted, "I'm home!"

Carol came into the living room and said, "You're late. Did you have another rough day at work again?"

"A little. Here, I got these for you," John said while holding out the flowers.

"For me? Thank you, honey! I haven't got flowers from you in a long time," Carol told him as she hugged him.

"I know. That's why I got them for you."

"How do I look?" Carol asked as she took a step back and twirled around to show John how she worked so diligently to make herself beautiful for him.

"That's a nice dress," John replied.

Carol was hoping for a little more specific compliment about herself, such as you look stunning and not just that the dress looked nice. However, a compliment in any form was still a rarity, so she was satisfied with it.

"I'll put these in a vase, and then I'll be ready to go," Carol said to John as she took the flowers to the kitchen.

"I'll wait for you in the car."

A few minutes later, Carol came rushing out of the house. The excitement of going to dinner with her husband was very apparent as she jogged across the front lawn.

"Where are we going to dinner?" Carol asked while being out of breath from the seventy-five-foot sprint to the car.

"I was thinking about trying that new Japanese restaurant that just opened up in Redondo, but since I got held up at work, it's probably best to eat at that steakhouse on Pier Ave."

"That would've been great to try something new, but steak does sound delicious," Carol said while still trying to catch her breath.

The steakhouse was just a few miles down the road, and it took less than twelve minutes to drive there. Twelve relatively peaceful minutes for John since Carol was still seemingly gasping for air and was unable to converse too much. The only other sound in the car was the radio that John turned the volume up on, attempting to drown out Carol's wheezing.

As they pulled into the parking lot, Carol dabbed the sweat from her forehead with a handkerchief she kept in her purse and checked her hair and makeup one last time in the visor mirror so she could look her best for John. John didn't bother to wait. He just got out of the car and made a beeline for the entrance. Carol tried to hurry her pace to catch up with him, but she barely made it halfway to the restaurant by the time John was already entering the door.

"Hi," the hostess greeted John. "Table for one?"

"No. there will be two of us. She's still making her way from the car."

The hostess curiously looked at John, wondering why he didn't walk in with his dinner guest like the gentleman he had the appearance of being.

A few seconds later, when Carol finally made her way into the restaurant, John said, "There she is. Do you have a table available for us?"

"Yes, I do have a table open. Follow me."

The three of them made their way through the narrow maze of walkways separating the tables. Carol took extra precaution not to embarrass herself or John by accidentally bumping into other diners.

"Will this table be sufficient?" the hostess asked as they stopped at a table in the middle of the restaurant.

"Actually, could we get that table in the back corner?" John inquired.

"Absolutely," the hostess said as she led the way.

The walkway seemed to narrow a bit more the further back they went, and despite Carol's best effort, she accidentally brushed against a couple of people and their table. She softly apologized and continued the arduous journey to her table, trying not to become a spectacle along the way.

"Here you are. Your waitress will be with you shortly," the hostess said as she placed the menus on the table and walked away.

"You must be starving," Carol said to John.

"Why do you say that?"

"Because of the way you rushed in here from the car."

"I did work through my lunch hour today," John replied.

"Well, let's get you some food. Excuse me." Carol said as she stopped a passing waiter.

"How can I help you, ma'am?"

"Could we get some dinner rolls, please?"

"Sure. I'll be right back with them."

"That should help you until our meals arrive," Carol told John.

"Thanks," John replied.

As John perused the menu, their waitress arrived at their table and stood behind John's left shoulder, trying to stay clear of another waiter serving food to a table across from them and said, "Hello, my name is Kayla. I will be serving you today."

John spun around and looked at the waitress as if he saw a ghost.

"I'm sorry, sir. Did I startle you?"

John quickly realized that it was not his Kayla. It just happened to be someone with the same name.

"A little," John replied.

"I apologize for that. Would you like to hear our specials, or do you already know what you would like?"

"I know exactly what I'm having," Carol said. "How about you, honey?"

"I believe we are ready to order," John told the waitress.

"What can I get you, ma'am?"

"I will have the petite sirloin, baked potato with butter on the side, and the vegetable medley."

"Very well. And for you, sir?"

"I'll have the Porterhouse steak, Baked potato with butter, sour cream, cheddar cheese, and bacon, and a Caesar salad with extra dressing."

"Excellent choice. Can I get either of you a drink from the bar?"

"I would love a glass of Merlot," Carol said.

"I'll just have an iced tea," John requested.

When the waitress left, Carol asked John, "Is everything okay with you?"

"I'm fine. Why?"

"You seemed a little frazzled when the waitress came over."

"It has been a long day. That's all."

John knew that was a thinly veiled excuse but hoped it would be sufficient to keep her from questioning him further and quash any suspicions Carol may have of what he has been up to lately.

"Here are your drinks and the dinner rolls you requested. Your dinners will be out shortly," the waitress informed them before heading to another diner's table.

"I love this table being in a quiet corner. It's very romantic," Carol told John.

"Romantic? Do you honestly think so?"

"Absolutely! Great choice, honey."

John was not trying to be romantic in the least. He selected that particular table because it was out of view from most patrons at the restaurant, which meant he could avoid people staring at Carol grazing on hordes of food and save himself some embarrassment.

Before long, the waitress brought them their dinners. Carol immediately cut her steak and baked potato in half and placed each half on her bread plate. John watched her curiously but never said a word. As a matter of fact, throughout the entire dinner, barely a word was spoken because Carol could see the look on John's face and how he would roll his eyes whenever she did try to talk to him, so she refrained from saying much.

When Carol finished the half portion of her meal on her dinner plate, she politely sat there sipping her wine and taking in the room's ambiance.

Noticing that half of Carol's meal remained on her bread plate, John asked, "Is there something wrong with your dinner?"

"Nothing is wrong with it. It was delicious."

"Are you feeling okay?" he asked.

"Yes. I feel great. Why do you ask?"

"I'm just wondering why you only ate half of your meal?"

"I decided to go on a diet," Carol proudly informed him.

"Good for you. When did you decide to do that?"

"This morning. I figured it was long overdue, and there's no time like the present to start it."

"I'm proud of you for taking the initiative to do that. I'm going to try to be as supportive as I can be for you."

John cleared his plate of every remaining morsel of food

as he always does. When the last bite entered his mouth, the waitress asked, "Could I interest either of you in a piece of cherry cheesecake? It is a specialty of our pastry chef and is made entirely from scratch."

"No, thank you. But I do need a box to take the rest of my dinner home," Carol said.

"I'd love a piece!" John told the waitress.

Carol cocked her head to the side and looked at him in disbelief that he would order that, knowing full well that she was on her first day of dieting.

"I'm sorry. That was rude of me." John apologized to Carol. "Can you please box up a piece to go for me? I'll eat it later at home."

It was a small effort on John's part to be supportive, but it was monumental as usual for Carol.

"Thank you, honey." Carol politely said as the waitress left.

"No problem. As I said, I'm going to be supportive. I know it isn't going to be easy for you to lose as much weight as you need to."

For most people, John's backhanded compliments and lack of empathy would anger or hurt them. However, Carol's self-esteem had been beaten down by him so far that she wouldn't know how to react if the man she so dearly loved just told her she was pretty without a barb attached.

A few minutes later, the waitress handed Carol a container for her leftover dinner then positioned herself in a manner next to Carol so she could lean in towards John as she opened the box with his cheesecake in it and asked, "What do you think?"

John stared unapologetically at her cleavage and said,

"Looks incredibly delicious." as he slowly rolled his eyes up from her chest to make eye contact with her.

The waitress gave him a little wink and a smile as she closed the lid of the box and placed the check on the table, which John promptly paid and told her to keep the change.

Carol paid little attention to what was transpiring in front of her. She was used to women flirting with John and figured this was just a shameless attempt at getting a bigger tip. Besides, she knew John would never blatantly try to get her phone number while she was with him, so the threat level was minuscule. She also knew there wasn't anything she could do about the situation anyway. If she did show jealousy, it would make John angry and drive him further away from her.

"Let's get out of here. It's still early enough that we can relax a couple of hours before bed." John told Carol.

"That sounds great!"

Carol, of course, was looking forward to spending a little more time with John. On the ride home, thoughts filled her head with all the things that they could do. They could snuggle on the couch and watch a movie. She could give him an erotic back rub. Or, if Carol dared to think it, even have sex. Four long months had passed since she last felt the tender touch of her lover's hand upon the most delicate areas of her flesh. She was starving for intimacy. Craving to feel the love and security of being embraced in his arms, to feel him inside her.

When they got home, Carol wrapped her arms around John, gave him a big hug, and said, "Thank you for dinner, honey. I'm going upstairs to put on something a little more comfortable."

John simply nodded his head and patted her on the back. Then, after arming himself with a fork from the kitchen, he sat down in his recliner and prepared to do battle with that delicious-looking cheesecake.

With every tasty bite and barely a breath between, John felt the walls of his stomach expand ever closer to capacity, but he was relentless in his determination to finish every bit of it. Once done, he tossed the empty container onto the end table, reclined his chair, and unbuttoned his pants to give himself a little relief from his now engorged stomach. If it were not for being blessed with such a high metabolism, John himself would be four hundred pounds due to his almost insatiable appetite.

Carol came downstairs in her favorite plush bathrobe that John gave her as a present last Christmas. She loved how the softness caressed her bare skin. She would rarely wear anything beneath it, and this evening was not any different.

"Did you find anything good to watch on the television?" Carol asked as she sat on the couch.

"I just turned it on and haven't looked for anything yet."

Carol grabbed the remote and started scrolling through the channel listing. For several minutes, every show and movie that she suggested got shot down by John with a no, that is a chick-flick, or there must be something better than that to watch. Finally, she found something they mutually agreed to. Well, at least for the most part. Carol was not a fan of action films but agreed to it because, for her, it was mostly about spending time with John and not about the movie itself.

As the movie began, Carol leaned against the arm of the

couch and turned towards John as she opened the top of her robe a bit wider, exposing her ample cleavage in temptation while asking John, "Why don't you come over here and sit on the couch with me?"

"I'm comfortable right where I am."

"Please. We haven't had a chance to watch a movie together in a long time. Come sit with me on the couch like you used to." Carol pleaded.

"I don't want to. I overate at dinner. I feel better laying back in my chair."

"You can lay down on the couch and put your head in my lap," Carol suggested.

John looked at her large, plump, pillowy thighs and thought, what the hell if it gets her to shut up so he can relax.

"Fine!" John huffed as he got up from his chair and begrudgingly made his way to the couch.

When John laid down with his head on her lap, she began to run her fingers gently through his silver hair.

Carol softly giggled and said, "The last time we did this, I could easily count the numbers of gray hairs you had. Now it would take me all night. Where does the time go?"

"I know. It has been a long time. Let's just watch the movie." John said as he reached up and patted her on the shoulder.

She continued massaging his scalp as they watched the movie, and within thirty-five minutes, John was fast asleep. Carol sat there looking at him and was amazed at how peaceful he appeared. The serene look on his face reminded her of how he used to be so many years ago. Long before their marriage problem surfaced, and agitation replaced his contentment.

Although Carol didn't want to, she continued watching the movie because John was a light sleeper and knew there was a possibility he would wake-up and retreat to his chair if the channel changed. Besides, she was content just being close to him, albeit with John asleep.

Carol reached down to John's hand that was tucked under his chin and gently cradled it in hers. Tears began to well up in her eyes because something like that was such a simple act of affection that John would not or seemingly could not do while he was awake. She so desperately missed his touch.

With the movie ending and sleepiness overtaking her, Carol carefully slid out from under John, making sure not to disturb his sleep. She then retrieved a pillow from the guestroom and eased it under his head. After covering him with a blanket from the back of the couch, she gently kissed John goodnight on his forehead, then went to bed herself.

As usual, when morning came, Carol awoke and started preparing for the day before the sun rose. The bangs and clangs of pots and pans emanating from the kitchen that John never heard while sleeping upstairs jarred him awake.

With his hand pressed firmly into the small of his back and slightly hunched over from the pain caused by sleeping on the couch, John walked into the kitchen as shouted, "What the hell are you doing? Do you know what time it is?"

"I'm making you breakfast. I always start at this time." Carol explained. "What's wrong with your back?"

"It hurts! That's what is wrong with it! Why didn't you wake me up to go to bed?"

"You were sleeping so peacefully I didn't want to disturb you. Here, let me give you a quick back rub." Carol offered as she took off her apron.

"No. I'll just soak in the tub."

"A back rub will make you feel better, honey." Carol insisted as she placed her hand on his back.

John immediately pulled away and yelled at her, "I said no!"

Carol jumped back from him, startled by his attitude. She wasn't used to his grumpiness in the mornings, even after seventeen years of marriage since they often woke up at different times. Usually, she didn't see or interact with him until after he was showered and fully awake.

"I'm sorry." Carol apologized.

"Leave me alone for a bit. I need to wake up and try to get rid of this backache by soaking in a hot bath." John said while stomping up the staircase.

Shortly after John had climbed into the tub, Carol softly knocked on the bathroom door.

"Yes," John said in an irritated tone.

"I brought you a cup of coffee," Carol said through the bathroom door.

"Okay. Come in."

Carol placed the cup on the edge of the bathtub and again apologized for not waking him up so he could come to bed.

"It doesn't matter. What's done is done. I just need to be left alone right now."

Carol went back downstairs and finished preparing his breakfast. At half-past six, John still had not come down to eat, but Carol was too nervous about disturbing him again by telling him that breakfast was ready.

Twenty minutes later, John came rushing down the stairs, immediately scolding her, "Why didn't you yell up to me that it was so late? Now I don't have time to eat!"

"You said that you wanted to be left alone. I didn't want to disturb you." Carol said in a sheepish voice.

John crammed a few bites of egg and a couple of spoonfuls of oatmeal into his mouth, then tucked his shirt into his pants.

"We need to get a damn clock in that bathroom," John grumbled as he wrapped a couple of pieces of bacon up in a napkin.

"There..." Carol suddenly stopped herself in mid-response. She knew she shouldn't dare tell him there is a clock on the wall opposite of where the sink is. That would only anger him further because he never noticed it.

"What? What were you going to say?"

"I'll pick one up today, honey."

"Okay. I have got to go." John said as he ran out the door without giving Carol a goodbye hug or kiss.

It was not quite the morning that Carol had hoped for after such an enjoyable evening. She had high hopes of keeping the love and affection flowing from last night, but she also understood that John was in pain and running late for work. The only thing she could do at this point was to hope that he has a good day and comes home in a better mood.

After cleaning up the breakfast dishes, Carol called Lisa to tell her about the lovely evening she shared with John.

"Hey, girl!" Lisa said, answering the phone. "How did it go last night?"

"It was wonderful. John brought me flowers, took me for a nice dinner, then we snuggled on the couch and watched a movie."

"No way! Really?" Lisa said in disbelief.

"Absolutely! He even requested a quiet, romantic table at the restaurant."

"Maybe I was wrong about John. Maybe there is some hope for him after all. Did you get laid last night?"

"Lisa!"

"What? I'm just asking."

"Well...no. John fell asleep shortly after he snuggled up on the couch with me."

"Damn. I suppose it's a start towards reconciliation on his part, but you need to get some loving. Hell, we know his junk still works since he's been getting it from other..."

"Stop!" Carol quickly interrupted Lisa. "Please don't bring that up. John and I are trying to move forward from all of that."

"You're right. Sorry. Hey, I have an early appointment at the office today, so I need to go. We can talk later. Okay?"

"Okay. Have a good day, Lisa."

"You too. Bye."

V

Chapter 5

The rest of the week carried on typically. There were no more flowers, restaurants, cuddling on the couch, or anything else that Carol could interpret as a romantic gesture from John. However, she continued to make his favorite foods and did her best to keep from pressuring him for affection, hoping that he would take the initiative to do it himself. Of course, Carol never did receive any such behavior from John. The one thing that she did find solace in was that he did come home directly from work every night. That alone was enough to keep Carol content, knowing that her husband was remaining faithful.

When John sat down for breakfast Friday morning, Carol decided to attempt scheduling more quality time with John over the weekend.

"I was thinking that since it's going to be perfect weather tomorrow, why don't we take a drive to Napa to do some wine tasting?" Carol asked.

"Tomorrow? I can't. I already made plans with Mike to go to the Dodgers game."

"Oh," Carol softly replied.

John could hear the disappointment in Carol's voice, so he offered her an alternative, "How about we have brunch Sunday and do a little antiquing instead."

"I would love that! You're the best, honey."

"Good. You do a lot for me around here, and it is the least I can do to show you that I appreciate it."

Carol was stunned that John gave her recognition for everything she did and didn't attach a negative comment as he usually does. That was the first time in many years that had happened. Carol didn't know what to say or how to react, so she simply asked, "Would you like another waffle?"

"No. I'm good. How's that diet of your going?"

"Seventy-two hours and still going strong." Carol proudly replied.

"I would've expected you to have given up by now."

"Nope. I am determined to shed this weight once and for all."

"I'm impressed so far, but it's going to be a long road to travel."

There is the typical John, Carol thought to herself. The one that always seems to enjoy knocking a person down a peg or two. Carol wished John would be supportive without the negativity. Without pointing out the considerable amount of weight she needs to lose, how long it will take, or that her previous attempts failed rather quickly. However, John was simply and unapologetically being himself.

"I know, honey. But I can do it. For me. For you. For us."

"Good luck with that. I better get to work."

"Have a good day!" Carol said as she began to clear the table.

When John got to work, he kept looking at his cellphone with an uncontrollable desire to call Kayla to see if she had Saturday off and was able to go to the ballgame. It was all he could think about, and his unproductive morning was evident of that.

Precisely at noon, John picked up his phone to call Kayla, but before he dialed, Mike walked into his office.

"I was thinking about heading over to Joey's Diner for lunch. Want to join me?" Mike asked.

"Sounds good. But I need to make a call first."

"Alright," Mike said as he sat down on the chair in the corner of John's office.

"It's a personal call," John said, indicating that he wanted some privacy.

"No problem. I'll meet you at the diner then."

When Mike was leaving, John asked, "Can you close the door for me?"

As soon as the door latched behind Mike, John started dialing Kayla's number. The phone rang several times before being sent to voicemail.

John left a message saying, "Hey, just checking to see if we were on for the game tomorrow. I'll call you back in about an hour." before hanging up the phone and catching up with Mike at the elevator.

"That was a quick call," Mike said.

"Yeah, the line was busy. I'll try again after lunch."

After arriving at the diner and placing their order, Mike

said, "I sure am looking forward to the game tomorrow. It has been a hell of a rough week, and I could use a little fun."

"I forgot to tell you that I may not be able to go to the game. I should know by the end of the day and will let you know as soon as I find out."

"You don't have to work, do you?" Mike asked.

"No. Something personal has come up that I'm trying to get taken care of. That's all. I know I always take you, but I hope you understand if I can't this time."

"Maybe we can get a round of golf in on Sunday then."

"No can do. I told Carol that I would take her shopping for antiques."

"You hate shopping. What did you screw up this time?"

"Nothing. Carol does a lot around the house, plus she's also on a diet and sticking to it. I figured it would be a nice reward for her effort."

"That's all? There isn't anything you're feeling guilty about or making up for? Just being nice?"

"Is that so hard to believe?" John inquired.

"Sometimes it is, John."

"Well, it's the truth."

"Have you talked to Kayla yet?" Mike asked.

"No. Why?"

"Just curious. Are you still going on a date with her?"

"I don't know. Why are you grilling me, Mike?"

"Just making conversation."

"Then let's talk about something else," John instructed Mike.

Lackluster work-related discussions filled the rest of their lunch hour before they headed back to the office. On the way back, John's phone rang; it was Kayla. John contemplated if he should answer it or not in front of Mike. He knew he wouldn't be able to speak freely with Kayla if Mike was within earshot without risking another lecture about his infidelities since it was apparent that Mike now sides with Peter on the issue. Nor did he want Mike to know that he was taking Kayla to the game instead.

"Are you going to answer that?" Mike asked.

"No, I'll call them back when I get to the office," John replied as he declined the call.

Immediately John's phone rang again. It seemed that Kayla wasn't going to stop calling until he answered the phone. He thought about silencing the ringer to avoid answering it in front of Mike, but he also didn't want Kayla to feel undesired by ignoring her call.

"Hello?" John reluctantly answered the phone.

"Hi, sexy!" Kayla said.

"What's up?"

"I'm returning your call."

"How did you get this number?" John asked.

"From caller ID, silly," Kayla told him.

"Of course."

John had invariably blocked his number in the past when calling a new woman in his life until he felt comfortable enough in their relationship to trust that they wouldn't attempt to contact him at inconvenient times. In his eagerness to find out about the possible date tomorrow, he forgot.

"Don't worry. I won't call you when you're at home." Kayla assured him.

"I'd appreciate that. What does your schedule look like?"

"I have the day off!"

"Fantastic! I'll call you when I get back to the office so we can finalize things."

"Finalize things? You're around someone and can't talk freely, can you?"

"That's correct."

"If you tell me that you want me right now, I will make Saturday one of the most memorable days of your life!" Kayla said.

John hesitated for a moment, looked at Mike out of the corner of his eye, and said, "I want you... to draw up the contract."

"That's cheating!" Kayla protested.

"No, it isn't."

"Besides, I said for you to say that you wanted me right now."

"I want you right now to draw up that contract."

"No! You are supposed to say those words. Not use them in a sentence."

"We'll discuss it later. I have to go." John said.

"Fine! Bye." Kayla said in a bratty tone.

"Who was that?" Mike asked as he pulled into his designated parking space.

John thought quickly and said, "Carter, from legal."

"Did you close a deal?"

"I'm trying to. Definitely trying to."

"I better get back to my office and finish things up. Let me know if we're going to the game when you know for sure. Good luck closing that deal."

"Thanks, but I won't be needing luck. I think it's in the bag." John said confidently.

As soon as John got back to the solidarity of his office, he called Kayla back.

"Hey," Kayla said, answering the phone.

"Hi, sexy lady. The game starts at four, so I figured I'd pick you up at two."

"That's fine. I'm so excited! I haven't been to a Dodgers game in a couple of years, and the seats were horrible. The upper deck in the outfield bleachers."

"You are in for a treat then. My seats are so close to the action that you can hear the footsteps of the players running to first base."

"That's awesome! I guess I'll see you at Sporty's at two then."

"Sure. Or I could pick you up at your place." John offered.

"Sporty's will be fine but thank you for the offer."

"Okay, I'll meet you there. See you tomorrow."

As John hung up the phone, a huge Cheshire cat grin appeared on his face. He knew that even if the Dodgers didn't score a single run, he was sure to score. Of course, he knew Kayla would make him work for it. However, to John, it would be undeniably worth the effort when the reward is a young, firm-bodied, gorgeous, blonde bombshell like Kayla.

A couple of hours later, John stopped by Mike's office to deliver the bad news saying, "It looks like I'm going to have to cancel the game with you tomorrow. I couldn't get things arranged to make it happen."

"I understand. What are you going to do with the tickets?" Mike asked, hoping that he could snag the seats.

"Uh, I'm giving them to my neighbor. He's going through a divorce and has been under a lot of stress at work. I figured it would do him some good to get out of the house and have a little fun."

"Huh," Mike uttered while silently wondering when John had become such a philanthropist since the few times he had done something nice for someone was because it happened to be a byproduct of getting what he wanted. "Well, I guess there's always next weekend."

"Next Saturday is an away game, but the Saturday after that, it's you and me, buddy!" John enthusiastically said, trying to ease Mike's disappointment.

"Sounds good."

"I have a couple of errands to run on my way home, so I'm heading out the door. Enjoy your weekend! I'll talk to you on Monday."

John drove to the sporting goods store to pick up a little something for Kayla. He wanted to make the day memorable for her. Since he was meeting her at a bar and going to a base-ball game, the standard fistful of flowers wouldn't be a fitting gesture. Instead, John decided on getting an official Dodgers jersey and hat and had it exquisitely gift wrapped.

John finished his shopping and toyed with the idea of stopping by Sporty's so he could watch that sexy young woman of his hustle from table to table while her hips swayed endlessly from side to side, and her breasts jiggled with every step she took. But he didn't want it to appear that he was too eager or possibly even stalking her. Besides that, there was also the possibility that Peter, Tony, or Mike could stop by there. So, to avoid bothering Kayla and possibly having to listen to another lecture from his friends, John drove home and continued playing the part of a faithful husband that he had become accustomed to portraying himself to be all week.

As soon as John walked into the house, Carol said, "Hi, honey. Perfect timing. Dinner will be ready in twenty minutes. How was your day?"

"Good." He replied as he tossed his keys on the table by the door.

"I hope you're hungry. I made baked salmon, wild mushroom and asparagus risotto, a spinach salad, and some homemade dinner rolls for you."

"Okay," John said as he plopped in his recliner.

"I talked to Mary today. She told me about..."

"Who?" John interrupted her in an irritated tone.

"Mary. Our neighbor across the street. Anyway, she told me about a quaint little antique shop in Huntington that I thought would be fun to look around in on Sunday. Then maybe we could have an early dinner at that Japanese restaurant in Redondo afterward."

"Whatever." John huffed as he got out of his chair and went to the kitchen to get a beer.

"Is everything okay, honey?" Carol asked.

"You know," John said as he popped the top to his beer and took a swig, "can't I have five minutes to myself when I come home before being smothered. I bust my ass all day long at work, and it would be nice to relax for five damn minutes."

"I'm sorry. Go ahead and relax. I'll call you when dinner is ready."

Fifteen minutes passed then Carol called John to the table for dinner. She didn't want to upset him further than he already was by speaking to him, so she patiently waited for John to initiate the conversation, which never happened. They sat there silently throughout dinner. When John finished, he got up from the table and retreated to the comfort of his recliner.

After Carol washed the dishes, she peered into the living room and noticed John watching a baseball game on the television. Having no desire to sit in silence and watch a sporting event that she had zero interest in, Carol opted to go to her bedroom. She took her knitting materials out of the closet, got cozy in her rocking chair, and attempted to pass the time by making a new blanket.

The usually enjoyable and straightforward task became challenging to concentrate on as she looked around her lonely bedroom where passion once thrived. Now it was just a room full of memories. Memories that become more painful for her with every passing night. A constant reminder of their broken marriage that she would give anything to be able to fix.

With tears welling in her eyes, Carol grabbed her phone and called Lisa.

"Hi, Carol. How are you doing, babe?"

Carol sniffled and said, "I just needed to hear a friendly voice."

"Did you and John get into another argument?"

"No. Not really."

"Then what's wrong?"

"I don't know. John came home, barely said a word to me, then he bit my head off for smothering him. I don't know what's wrong."

"Maybe he had a bad day at work." Lisa offered a possible explanation.

"He said he had a good day."

"Maybe it wasn't, and he doesn't want to talk about it."

"I suppose, but I've been married to him for over seventeen years, and he seems to be acting peculiar. More so than usual. One day he is romantic and thoughtful, and the next day he is completely unapproachable. I swear, if he hadn't been coming directly home every day from work this week, I'd think he was having another affair."

"You said it yourself, Carol. He has been coming home. He has been trying to be thoughtful. Maybe tomorrow will be a better day for both of you." Lisa tried to console her friend even though she didn't trust John enough to believe what she was saying herself.

"You're right. Maybe I am reading too much into things." Carol said.

"Now, I didn't say that. I'm just offering you another possibility for why John is acting the way he is. You know I do not trust that man, and if you say something is wrong, I believe you. I'm only trying to calm you down. Let's see what tomorrow brings before either of us jumps to conclusions."

"Okay. Thanks for being there for me, Lisa."

"That's what friends do. Now get some rest and call me tomorrow."

VI

Chapter 6

Saturday morning, John came trotting down the stairs, whistling a cheerful tune.

"You're in an excellent mood this morning," Carol noted.

"That I am," John replied as he grabbed Carol's hand, twirled her around, pulled her close to him, and kissed her on the forehead. "The weather is perfect, and it is going to be a great baseball game."

"I don't know what got into you, but I like it," Carol said with a smile.

"What's for breakfast?" John asked as he sat down at the table and opened the newspaper.

"I haven't started anything yet," Carol said while bringing John his coffee. "What would you like?"

The image of Kayla sprawled out across the kitchen table immediately came to the forefront of his thoughts.

"There are so many things I would like, but for breakfast, I'll have eggs, sausage, and toast."

Carol worked feverishly to prepare John's breakfast. Since

he was inherently an impatient man, the quicker the food was ready for John, the better the chance she had to keep him in this good mood. In near-record time, she placed his breakfast in front of him, complete with hash browns covered in gravy, a guilty pleasure of John's.

"Doesn't that look delicious," John said as he folded up the newspaper.

Putting aside the paper was a monumental sign that he was in a rare, jubilant mood. John almost always kept his face buried in it to avoid being forced into conversation with Carol, so she immediately sat down at the table with him.

"Aren't you going to eat?" John asked.

"I had half of a grapefruit earlier."

"Still on that diet, huh?"

"I am. I've lost five pounds this week." Carol informed him with a beaming smile, proud of her achievement.

"Congratulations!"

"Thank you, honey."

"Have you decided where you want to go shopping tomorrow?"

Carol wasn't surprised that John didn't remember what she had told him last night. She knew he wasn't truly listening to her.

"There's a place in Huntington I'd like to go to."

"Huntington it is then! Hey, how about we go to that Japanese restaurant in Redondo afterward. Can you have that on your diet?"

Carol was astonished by John's thoughtfulness even though she had brought up the same idea yesterday.

Knowing the best way to a man's heart was to inflate his

ego, Carol said, "That sounds fantastic, and yes, I can have that on my diet. You have the best ideas, honey."

John winked his eye at Carol and continued eating his breakfast. When he finished, John dabbed his mouth with a napkin and said, "I better get going. I want to get the car detailed before picking up Mike."

"But it's only nine o'clock." Carol protested, hoping to prolong the enjoyable morning she was having with him.

"I told Mike I would pick him up at two, and you never know how long the detail shop is going to take, how traffic will be, or how hard it will be to find a spot to park at the Stadium. I don't want to be late for the game, you know."

"I guess you should go then. Have fun. Go Dodgers!" Carol cheered.

John's giddiness continued throughout the time it took to get his car washed and the seemingly more distant than usual drive to Sporty's. It was as if going on a date with Kayla was amongst the most significant achievements in his life. More incredible than when John got into Harvard Business School and landed his first six-digit salary job. Up to this point in his life, everything he had accomplished paled in comparison to the prospect of having Kayla as a possible permanent attachment on his arm.

He truly knew very little about Kayla, but an undeniable attraction shared between them went more in-depth than the typical superficial appearances that attracted John to most women. When they were together, it was as if she was the missing piece to his soul that made him feel complete. John couldn't pinpoint what it was that drew him to her with such a magnetic pull, just that it was different with her than it had been with anyone else he had ever known. All the previous women were mere conquests that satisfied his carnal urges and reaffirmed his manhood, but his desires for Kayla were on a much more profound level.

Arriving at the bar ninety minutes early, John decided to go in and have a drink or two while waiting for Kayla. As he took a seat at the bar, a familiar voice within the background noise caught his attention. John turned to his right and slowly scanned the room for the location of that unmistakable sound.

John spotted Kayla sitting in the bar's back corner with a few friends. He was mesmerized watching her. The radiant smile on her face and the animated gestures she made with her hands while talking displayed her energetic and passionate zest for life. It is a quality that attracted John to her as much if not more than her sex appeal did.

John examined Kayla from a distance for ten minutes before being spotted by her. Her eyes lit up as she rushed over to hug him.

"You're early," Kayla said.

"So are you," John replied.

"I'm just so excited about going to the game and didn't want to be late, which I usually am," Kayla confessed. "What's your excuse?"

"I was just excited to see you."

"You're the sweetest man I know."

"Stay right here. I have to get something from the car." John instructed her before he went to retrieve Kayla's present.

Upon John's return, Kayla hopped off the barstool and asked, "Is that for me?"

"Yes, it is. Go ahead and open it."

Kayla tore into the gift like a kid on Christmas morning. When she pulled the jersey and hat from the box, she exclaimed, "I love it! Thank you." and kissed John on the cheek. "Number 12 too. How did you know Williams was my favorite player?"

"It was an educated guess. He's the favorite player of ninety percent of the female fans."

"He is so hot!" Kayla gushed. "I mean not as hot as you, but hot. You know, for a baseball player."

"It's okay. I know what you mean." John chuckled.

"I'm going to put it on. I'll be right back." Kayla said as she took her gift to the employee locker room.

Kayla slipped into the jersey, pulled her hair back into a ponytail that she fed through the opening at the back of the hat, then returned to John for his inspection.

"What do you think?"

"Incredible. Simply incredible."

"I'm glad you approve. Let's go back to the table where my friends are so I can introduce you and show you off a little." Kayla said with a grin.

"Sure, we have a little time yet before we have to leave."

Kayla took John by the hand, and they snaked through the mass of people showing up early to watch the game at the bar.

"Guy's, this is my friend John. He's taking me to the Dodgers game this afternoon." Kayla proudly informed her friends. "John, these are my friends Allison, Beth, and Mark."

John felt the blood drain from his face and his stomach knotted up into a ball when he recognized Mark from the Christmas party Carol hosted at their house last year. Lisa's daughter invited her boyfriend to attend the party with her, and that boyfriend happens to be Mark.

"Have we met before?" Mark asked John.

"No, I don't believe we have. I'm fairly good with faces and would probably remember if we had."

"You look familiar," Mark said curiously. "Where did you and Kayla meet?"

"We met here," Kayla answered for John.

"That's probably why I look familiar to you. You recognize me from the bar."

"No. That can't be it. It's my first time here."

"Well, don't rack your brain too hard. It's probably just mistaken identity. As I said, I don't forget a face."

"Why don't you two sit down and have a drink with us," Allison suggested.

"I'll grab an extra chair," Kayla said.

John quickly grabbed Kayla by her arm and pulled her back to his side while saying, "Actually, we have to get going. There's going to be a lot of traffic getting to the stadium."

"Bummer. Maybe next time." Beth said.

"Definitely. It was nice meeting everyone," John said, then he made a beeline for the exit with Kayla in tow.

When they got outside, Kayla asked, "What got into you? We have time for a drink."

"It's Mark. We have met each other before."

"Then why did you say you didn't remember him. He clearly remembers you from somewhere."

"He's dating the daughter of my wife's best friend."

"Oh, I see."

"Yeah, if he figured out who I am, there's going to be hell to pay because it will most definitely get back to my wife."

"I don't think you have anything to worry about, Mark's cool. I doubt he would say anything." Kayla tried to assure John.

"I don't want to take the chance. I hope you understand."

"I do. Let's head to the stadium. We can grab some beers there. Where are you parked?"

"This is mine," John said, pointing to his Dodge Challenger Hellcat.

"Wow. Awesome!"

"Thanks. I like it. I traded in the BMW M4 I had last year. It was a great car, but this is a wild ride. Over seven hundred horses under the hood." John said as he fired up the thunderous motor.

"You wear designer clothes, a Rolex watch, Live in Hermosa Beach, have season tickets to the Dodgers, and a bitchin' ride? Amazing."

"What can I say? I guess I have impeccable taste in everything." John said with a wink.

"What do you want with a waitress from Pasadena? You can have anyone you want."

John smiled and shook his head in amazement. He could not believe she noticed the elegance of his possessions but that she couldn't see her own grandeur. Or how, for a man that had virtually everything he has ever wanted, she was the one thing that had eluded his every attempt to obtain. The vibrant, beautiful, young piece of arm-candy that would make him the envy of all men. According to John, there isn't a car manufactured, a suit tailored, or a house built that could convey the level of success a man had achieved in life better than the woman beside him.

Finally arriving at the stadium, John and Kayla got a couple of beers before heading to their seats, where they continued getting to know one another. However, when the first pitch was ready to be thrown, the conversation abruptly ended, and Kayla's relaxed seating posture changed to a more attentive position on the edge of her seat.

Kayla clapped, yelled, and whistled as the Dodgers got hit after hit, but she was not shy about being vocal when they committed an error or struck out either.

"Jennings, you suck!" Kayla shouted when the second-best player on the roster took strike three at the plate. "How can a guy with a .360 batting average strike out against a pitcher with a 3.8 ERA?" she asked John rhetorically.

John was in awe of Kayla's in-depth knowledge of baseball. He had always dreamt about sharing his passion for the sport with an incredible woman like her but never thought he would find it.

Over the next couple of hours, they barely spoke about anything that didn't have something to do with the game, but they still had a great time watching the Dodgers win 6-0 and secure a place in their division for the playoffs.

"That was a fantastic game! Thanks for bringing me." Kayla said in a slightly raspy voice from all the shouting she did.

"It was my pleasure. Maybe we can do this again. You can come to one of the playoff games with me if you want to."

"Hell yeah, I would love that!" Kayla exclaimed.

"Then it's a date."

"I suppose we better head back to the bar. I don't want you to get grounded for coming home late." Kayla jokingly said.

When they got back to Sporty's, the place was packed with people still celebrating the big win.

"Would you like to come in and have a drink with me?" Kayla asked John.

John quickly scanned the parking lot to see if he recognized any of the vehicles there before saying, "Sure, I can hang out for a bit."

That one drink quickly turned into several. Before John knew it, it was one o'clock in the morning.

"It's getting pretty late, and I have a busy day tomorrow. I better head home." John told Kayla.

"If you have to. I'm going to stay a little longer." Kayla said, downing another shot.

As John stood up from the bar, he asked, "When is your next night off? Maybe we can get together for dinner."

Kayla spun around on the barstool to face John and motioned with her index finger for him to lean in closer. As he did, Kayla threw her arms around his neck, wrapped her legs around his waist, and passionately kissed him.

The firm pressing together of their lips and gentle flicking of their tongues aroused both more than they could have anticipated. There was a charge of energy transferring from one another, feeding their hungry souls that were now intertwined after lifetimes apart.

John stood upright with Kayla still clinging to him as their hips began to voraciously grind against one another in a display of their animalistic desires as their tongues spoke clearly of what they wanted without uttering a single syllable.

More intoxicating than all the alcohol they had consumed, the kiss they shared seemed to transport them to another dimension where only the two of them existed. There were no worries, cares, or spouses that concerned them, just pure unbridled passion. But it was not long before the howls and cat-calls from the voyeuristic patrons snapped them back from the trancelike lust they were engaged in.

John slowly sat Kayla down on the bar's counter and put a small distance between them to hush the vocal crowd, quelling their hope of a more pornographic display of affection.

"Damn, that was hot! Are you sure you have to leave?" Kayla asked.

"I don't want to. I really don't want to, but I have to."

"I'm throwing myself at you, and you're still going to leave?" Kayla asked as she hopped off the bar. "Don't tell me you suddenly found some morals or have some kind of aversion to sleeping with a woman on the first date."

"That's not it. I probably want it more than you do, but I made some promises that I have to keep. Otherwise, I would stay all night with you."

"This sucks," Kayla whined.

"I know it does, and I will make it up to you. I promise."

"You better!"

"I will. I'll call you soon." John said, then gave her a smaller, gentler kiss than the previous one, but none less intoxicating.

With tongues again twirling in each other's mouth, Kayla took John's hand and, as discreetly as possible, slid it under her jersey. John became more aroused as his hand caressed her supple breast, making going home an almost unbearable thought.

Kayla softly moaned in John's ear as he began playing with her erect nipples. Her teeth gently raking against his earlobe filled John with an uncontrollable urge to make love to her.

"Let's get a room at the hotel across the street. I need to feel you inside me." Kayla panted.

John slid his hand from under her jersey and said, "Please don't make this any more difficult than it already is for me. You know I want you. There isn't anything in this world that I want more than to make love to you, but I do have to go home."

"You can't blame a girl for trying," Kayla said as she hopped off the counter.

While John and Kayla were on their secret date, Carol worked diligently to finish her weekend household duties to ensure she could enjoy shopping with John on Sunday. It was difficult for Carol to relax if there was something left undone. Hence, it was of utmost importance to check everything off her weekend to-do list.

Around five o'clock, Carol's phone rang.

"Hello?"

"Hey, Carol. It's Mike. Is John there? I tried calling his cell-phone, but he hasn't answered it all afternoon."

"No, he told me he was going to the ball game with you," Carol said, confused by Mike's call.

There was silence on the phone as Mike realized that John had lied not only to Carol but to him as well, and he quickly tried to think of a way to backpedal out of the predicament he just got himself into.

"Uh, something came up at the last minute that made it so I couldn't go to the game. I figured John didn't go either because you know how he hates to go to the games alone. But it is an important game, so I guess he did end up going. Alone." Mike stumbled around his explanation.

"I guess he did," Carol said. "I'll be sure to let him know you called."

"Thanks. Bye." Mike said, rushing to get off the phone.

Carol knew John better than to believe Mike's story. John had not gone to a baseball game alone in over ten years. Rather than going alone, John would coerce her into going even though he was more than aware of her indifference towards sports. Sometimes he would even take someone new from work, but he would not go alone.

She didn't want to jump to conclusions and think the worst, but John's track record would suggest that the worst was the most plausible explanation. Still, Carol racked her brain to think of any other rational answer possible to vindicate John. Every one of which Carol tried to come up with sounded precisely like a scripted and well-rehearsed excuse that John himself would come up with, and that didn't sit well with her. It isn't like Carol to have a pessimistic frame of mind, and she despises thinking in such a manner, but it is who John is forcing her to become.

As night fell, the fear of John having another affair gained a stranglehold on her. Carol sat motionless in the dark on the couch, lost in her thoughts, without bothering to turn on a light. It was times like this that she would search every corner of her mind to find a happy memory to hold onto to elevate her feelings of despair. However, she wasn't successful this time. Instead, Carol analyzed every joyful memory, questioning how real they were or if those times were just a façade put there by John to conceal his extramarital activities. She asked herself if he ever did love her or just loved what she did for him and wondered why he stayed married to her if he preferred to be with other women.

The vast emptiness and deafening quietness of the darkness overtaking the room seemed to emanate from within her. The haunting of broken dreams and shattered hopes that tormented Carol every day faded away into the blackness of the night, giving her eerily peaceful contentment. It was then that she began noticing a similarity between John and that darkness. They both seemed cold and lifeless, void of any emotion towards her, and they both appear to show what they are yet at the same time harbor hidden secrets from within.

Every hour after agonizing hour passed as Carol continued to ponder the many thoughts racing through her head until the sound of John entering the side door broke her concentration, but she didn't say a word to alert him of her presence.

John made his way to the living room, turned on the table lamp, and was startled by Carol's presence.

"Damn it, Carol. What the hell are you doing sitting in the dark?"

"Just waiting for you, darling."

Trying his best not to focus on Carol's odd behavior, John shook his head, turned on the television, and went to the kitchen to get a beer.

"Did you and Mike have a good time at the game? That is who you took, isn't it?" Carol asked, baiting the trap to catch him in a lie, then threw in a couple more questions to avoid it being too obvious about what she knew. "Did they win? What was the score? You didn't bet anything with Mike on the game, did you? I know how the two of you are when it comes to baseball."

John was perplexed by Carol's line of questioning. She was fully aware of who he said he was taking to the game. Carol had never asked about the score before either. And what was she doing sitting in the dark like that? Something was amiss, and he better figure it out quickly.

"I can't hear you. Hold on a second." John said, checking his cellphone and noticed five missed calls from Mike and a text message that read, 'Call ASAP before you get home.' Which indicated to John that something had transpired, possibly bringing to light his deceit.

"I asked if you and Mike had fun at the game," Carol repeated herself as she walked into the kitchen.

John casually slipped his cellphone into his pocket and said, "Mike backed out at the last minute, so I went to the game by myself."

"You went alone?" Carol questioned.

"Yes. Alone. It was a last-minute thing. I knew Tony and Peter already had plans, so I went alone."

"Then why are you getting home so late?" Carol continued to interrogate him for that gotcha moment when she could confront him with evidence of an affair.

"I had a few drinks at the bar. I didn't know I had to call home to ask for permission." John said snidely.

John's cynical disposition was all it took to flip a switch inside Carol. The demure housewife became an assertive scorned woman that refused to accept the status quo of believing his dishonesty simply to make it through another day.

"You never go to the game alone, John. Ever!"

"Are you accusing me of something, Carol? Are you?" John shouted in her face. "Because I have come home every day right after work. I've taken you to dinner, made plans to take you shopping tomorrow, and just because I go to one baseball game alone, you think I'm screwing someone! Is that it, Carol?"

"Who did you go to the game with, John, or did you even go?" Carol persisted in her search for answers.

"I don't need this crap. This conversation is over!"

"It's not over until you tell me what's going on."

"I'm leaving," John said as he grabbed his keys.

"Where are you going? Are you going to your little whore's house?" A defiant Carol asked, not backing down an inch.

"I can't believe you. You have lost your mind. You have finally gone off the deep end."

"Where, John? Where are you going?"

"I don't know. Maybe I'll get a hotel room. I'm just not going to put up with your harassment tonight."

"Good! Maybe you can call your girlfriend and have her come over for another fling."

"How many times do I have to tell you, Carol. I am not sleeping with anyone. I could have if I wanted to, but no, I came home to you."

"So, you are seeing someone, aren't you?"

"I am done discussing this. I'm done with your accusations. I don't deserve to be treated this way. I admit I have made some mistakes in the past. Who hasn't? But that doesn't give you the right to hold an inquisition just because you feel insecure."

The thought ran through Carol's mind that maybe John was right. It could be possible that this is just her insecurities running rampant. He has been good to her and appeared to be trying since the last time he made a mistake. Maybe her emotions did get the better of her.

"I'm sorry, honey," Carol said. "You're right. I love you so much and can't bear the thought of losing you."

As Carol approached John to hug him, he backed away from her and said, "I need to cool down. I'm going for a drive."

"Are you coming back?"

"I don't know, Carol. I am so upset with you right now."

"I'm sorry," Carol said as John left out the door.

John sat in his car, relieved that he was able to deflect her suspicions of an affair. Over the next fifteen minutes, John sat in his car as he carefully planned his next move while Carol peered out of the bedroom window, watching to see if he was going to leave. He knew if he left for the night, it would almost solidify her suspicions or at the least give her reason to suspect further that he was spending the night with another woman, so that option was off the table. The best thing for him to do was go back inside, go to bed, and forgive Carol in the morning. That way, it would reinforce Carol's thinking that the argument was her fault and keep her from bringing up the topic for at least a little while, fearing that he may not be so forgiving next time.

When John made his way back into the house, Carol quickly climbed into bed so it wouldn't appear evident that she was worried if he was going to leave or not. She laid there

in the darkness that has seemingly become an all too familiar companion of hers. Eventually, John did come to the bedroom, changed his clothes, and climbed into bed on the very
edge just as he had always done.

That satisfied Carol. It was not passionate makeup sex or
even a simple cuddle until they fell asleep, but she knew the
man that she loved had chosen to stay home with her, and
that was enough.

VII

Chapter 7

The following day John woke up to his empty bed as usual, but when he came downstairs, instead of finding Carol in the Kitchen with coffee brewed and breakfast cooking, he saw her on the couch, still in her robe staring at the wall.

"Don't tell me you're still mad about last night," John said, preparing for round two of the argument.

Carol didn't respond or acknowledge John's presence in the least, though it wasn't out of anger. She was merely quietly lost in an emotional sea of thoughts and oblivious to her surroundings.

"Carol!" John shouted.

Her head turned toward John, but her eyes seemed to fail to recognize that he was standing right beside her.

"What the hell is wrong with you?" he asked.

Carol snapped out of the trance she was in and said, "Good morning, honey. You're up early. I'll make some coffee."

"What are you talking about? It's nine o'clock."

"Surely it isn't that late." She said, walking into the kitchen.

After filling the coffee maker with water and freshly ground coffee, Carol paused in mid-motion with her finger hovering over the brew button as she noticed the clock on the coffee maker. It was then that she realized John was indeed correct about the time.

Fear swept over her as she tried to recall the last four hours but couldn't come up with a logical rationale other than that she was losing her mind. She remembered waking up and coming downstairs, so she wasn't sleepwalking. However, she had no idea what transpired between then and when John yelled at her.

John came into the kitchen to check on Carol and found her hunched over the counter and staring at the coffee maker. He curiously watched for a moment as she appeared to be a life-sized wax figure of his wife. Motionless and fake, but uncannily realistic.

"Are you okay?" John asked.

Carol again snapped back to reality and said, "I guess I'm just not feeling well."

"Have you had anything to eat this morning? Maybe your blood sugar is low."

"I don't know," Carol replied in a bewildered tone.

"What do you mean you don't know? How can you not remember if you have had anything to eat?"

Carol shrugged her shoulders and shook her head as she got the mugs out of the cabinet.

"Just get dressed. We can stop for breakfast on our way to Redondo." John told her.

"If you don't mind, I would rather stay home today."

"Really? I made sure to schedule time with you today. Now you don't want to go. Are you sick?"

"No, I don't know what is wrong with me. I'm feeling a little confused but not ill."

"Confused about what?"

"I don't know. Nothing. Everything. I'm going to lay down in bed." Carol said, trying to explain what she couldn't understand herself before going back to bed.

With John's entire day free, he decided not to let it go to waste and headed to the country club for a round of golf.

When he arrived there, John popped the trunk lid so the caddy could unload his clubs, handed a twenty-dollar bill to the valet attendant, and said, "Keep it away from the third hole. There are way too many errant shots over there."

"Yes, sir!" the valet said as he slid the big tip into his pocket.

As John walked towards the clubhouse, he stopped in his tracks when he saw Mike and Peter standing by the door talking. John contemplated turning around and leaving because he didn't want to explain to Mike what happened last night. Still, before he could decide what to do, Tony came out of the clubhouse and noticed John.

"Hey, John!" Tony shouted.

"What's up, guys?" John responded, trying to act like he didn't notice them before. "Are you guys heading out onto the course or finishing up?"

"We're heading to the tee box. We'll wait for you." Tony said.

"Hey, what happened yesterday? I tried calling you, but

you never answered, so I got hold of Carol thinking maybe your phone had died. Carol said you went to the game." Mike inquired.

"Long story. I'll tell you about it later. Tony, you're riding with me today, so I can make sure you don't cheat."

It was an unusual request because Mike always rode with John but having Tony in the cart kept Mike from adamantly pressing him for information. At least for the time being.

"Okay, but you're still going to lose," Tony told John.

"Are you sure enough of that to play for five dollars a hole?" John asked.

"You're on!"

After three hours on the golf course, the guys tallied the scores, and Tony ended up being the big winner of the day.

"Thank you, gentlemen," Tony said as he put his winnings in his wallet. "Let me tell you that since I am such a gracious winner, let's go get some beers, and I'll buy the first few rounds."

"Sounds good to me," John said, happily accepting the invitation.

"Count me in," Mike said.

"Not me," Peter said. "I appreciate the offer, but I'm going back home."

"Come on," Tony insisted. "You're going to give up free beer?"

"Let's see. I can have a couple of beers with a few guys, or I can go home and chase my wife around the bedroom for a couple of hours. Hmm. I'm definitely going home. No offense, guys. But she is a lot hotter than any of you."

"Alright. I guess I'll meet you two at Sporty's." Tony said.

"Sporty's? Why not grab some beers here at the club?" John asked Tony.

"Because it's too pretentious here. Besides, I know Sporty's will have the Cubs game on." Tony told him.

"What's wrong with Sporty's, John?" Mike asked.

"Nothing. I thought we could save some time and drink here."

"Do you have to be somewhere anytime soon?" Tony asked.

"No," John admitted.

"Good. It's settled. I'll see you guys at Sporty's."

On the drive to the bar, John kept hoping that Kayla wouldn't say anything about going to the game yesterday. He wasn't embarrassed about it in the least, but he did want to keep things discreet for the time being. Especially since he still needed to come up with a good excuse to tell Mike for ditching him.

As the guys walked into Sporty's, Kayla immediately noticed them and motioned them to her section.

"Good to see you guys! I'll clear off this table, and you can sit here." She said before heading to the back with a handful of dishes.

When Kayla returned, she stood beside John, bumped his shoulder with her hip, and said, "What's going on, sexy?"

"Not much. How are you, beautiful?" Tony said.

Kayla smirked at Tony and rolled her eyes.

"Oh, you were talking to John."

"Yeah, I was. What can I get you guys?"

"We'll have a round of beers on me." Tony proudly said.

"Okay, big spender! I'll be right back with them."

When she walked away, Mike sternly glared at John.

"What?" John asked.

"You didn't, did you?" Mike asked, insinuating that John took Kayla to the game.

"No, of course not," John said, denying the accusation.

"Bull!"

"What's going on, guys?" Tony asked.

"John took Kayla to the Dodgers game yesterday instead of me! Worse yet, he lied about going himself."

"No, I did not." John protested.

"There's one way to find out," Tony said as Kayla made her way back to the table. "Kayla, you're a Dodgers fan. Did you see the game yesterday?"

"Hell yeah. I actually went to it." Kayla said as John slid down in his seat.

"You did?"

"Yeah. John has some great seats. It was amazing! Let me know if you guys need anything else." Kayla said as she hustled to the next table.

"Okay, so I took her to the game." John conceded.

"It's bad enough that you ditched your so-called best friend to take a woman on a date to the game, but then to top it off, you lied about it."

"What do you expect me to do? The way you and Peter have had this holier than thou attitude about me taking her out, I had to keep it quiet."

"Holier than thou?" Mike asked.

"Yeah. The two of you act like I'm committing murder or something."

"I've kept my mouth shut about every affair you've had, John. But you know something, I've never cheated on any of the girlfriends I've had, and Peter has never cheated on Lauren. So, in that respect, I guess we are better than you." Mike told him.

"Well, congratulations!" John said sarcastically while clapping his hands. "I guess you both are in the running for Man of the Year!"

"Let's not start fighting, guys." Tony pleaded.

"You made a vow to remain faithful to Carol the day you married her, yet you keep cheating on her. She has forgiven you what, four or five times now?"

"So what? She isn't going anywhere. She knows she will never get another man like me."

"You mean another man that would cheat on her?"

"Keep your nose out of my marriage, Mike. It doesn't concern you."

"Carol may not say anything to you, but I can't look the other way any longer. You're an ass, John."

"Screw you!"

"Guys, stop," Tony begged.

"Thanks for the beer Tony, but I'm going to go home," Mike said as he got up to leave.

"Mike, please stay. Let's change the subject." Tony said, trying to calm the tension.

"Just let him go," John told Tony as Mike headed out the door.

"This isn't how I expected today to turn out."

"Sorry about that, Tony. But you understand, don't you?"

"Understand what?"

"If you had an opportunity to go on a date with a woman

like Kayla, you would cancel your plans with me for her, wouldn't you?"

"In a New York second!"

"Thank you," John said, feeling vindicated for his actions.

"But I wouldn't lie to you about it, and I sure wouldn't cheat on my wife if I were married."

John took a swig of his beer then said, "That's a crock of crap, Tony, and you know it."

"Don't get me wrong. I would be tempted. I'd even have more than a couple of fantasies about it, but I wouldn't be able to follow through with it. That's one of the best parts of having you as my friend, John. I can live vicariously through you."

"You don't think I'm an ass for doing what I did?"

"No way! You're just doing what other guys wish they had the guts to do."

"Thanks, Tony. I'm glad one of my friends understands."

"Understands what?" Kayla said as she brought a round of shots to the table.

"Understands how lucky I am to have you in my life," John said.

"Awe. You know all the right things to say to a girl, don't you?" Kayla gushed. "Where's Mike? I brought everyone a round of shots on me."

"He had to go home rather unexpectedly," John replied.

"Yeah. Mike couldn't hang with the big boys, could he John?"

"You don't mind if I have his shot then, would you?" Kayla asked.

"Help yourself. You bought the shots." John told her.

Kayla knocked back the shot and grabbed John's bottle of beer for a quick chaser.

"Damn, that's some good stuff. Too bad I'm on the clock, I'd love to sit and hang out with the two of you, but I better get back to work."

"Before you go, this should cover our tab," Tony said, handing her some cash.

"You guys are leaving already?"

"Yeah, at least I am," Tony said.

"What about you, stud?" Kayla asked John.

"What time do you get off work?"

"Today, I don't get off work until ten."

"Damn. Yeah, I guess I'm going to take off too."

"Alright. Call me sometime. Maybe we can finish what we started in here last night." Kayla told John.

"Absolutely! Let's go, Tony."

On the way to the parking lot, Tony could not resist the temptation of finding out what got started last night and asked, "What was she talking about in there? What happened last night?"

"Nothing much. I better get going. Carol has been acting strange, and I'm sure she hasn't prepared anything for dinner. So, I'm going to grab some Chinese food on my way home."

"But aren't you going to tell me what happened last night?"

"I'll leave it up to your imagination for now. We'll talk later."

John stopped on his way home to pick up dinner as he said he was going to, and he even grabbed enough food for Carol as well. Since Carol had just recently started acting odd, he figured maybe it had something to do with her diet. Her eating something may be the cure to normalize his home life.

As he walked into the silent and darkened house due to Carol never opening the blinds, John called out for her to find out where she was lurking to avoid being startled by her yet again.

"Carol, I'm home."

"Honey, is that you?" Carol shouted back from upstairs.

"Yeah. I picked up some Chinese food. Come down and eat with me."

"No. I'm not hungry. You enjoy it."

"Carol, you need to come down here and eat. This diet of yours is messing up your blood sugar, and you are not thinking clearly. Get down here now and have some dinner."

"I'm on a diet," Carol shouted to John.

"You can start dieting again once you feel better."

Carol came downstairs and told John, "I'm already starting to feel better. I think it was only exhaustion that was making me feel peculiar. I probably overextended myself with all the chores I did yesterday, trying to get everything done."

"Regardless, I still want you to eat."

"I'll nibble on some rice, but seriously, I'm not hungry enough for a full meal."

John and Carol sat down for dinner. As usual, John devoured his food and was soon sitting in his recliner watching television. In contrast, Carol sat alone in the kitchen, picking at the plate of food John had prepared for her.

Little by little, Carol started getting that familiar comfort she had always got with food. Each bite she took made her feel more at ease. Soon Carol began inhaling her food, reminiscent of the way John eats.

Twenty minutes later, Carol came into the living room and told John, "Thank you, honey. You were right. I think it was my diet getting to me. I feel much better now."

"I figured that's what it was. Glad you're feeling better, but I would like to finish watching this show if you don't mind."

"Okay. I'll sit here on the couch and watch it with you. I promise to be quiet so you can enjoy it. I just wanted to thank you for being there for me. I'll make it up to you tomorrow with a special dinner."

"That would be nice. Now, hush."

They sat there watching television without uttering a word to each other. Carol would slyly glance over at him during commercial breaks, but she never asked him what he was thinking.

About an hour later, Carol began to feel sad and alone, which confused her since they were in the same room, watching the same show, yet she felt miles apart from him. So, she did what had always helped her feel better in the past. Carol went to the kitchen and finished off the leftovers in the refrigerator. After the wave of contentment washed over her from her now engorged stomach, she returned to the living room.

"I think I'm going to call it a day and head to bed. It's going to be a crazy week, and I need to get some rest." John told Carol.

"Sweet dreams, honey. I'm going to stay up for a little longer."

It was bizarre that she would stay up later than he did,

but John didn't say a word about it. Instead, there seemed to be an extra joyous bounce to his step as he went upstairs. It was the first time in nearly a decade that he would be able to fall asleep in bed without having to grit his teeth through her dreadful snoring.

John laid there with a big grin on his face relishing the peacefulness of the room. However, falling asleep proved to be more of a chore than expected as it was too quiet. After all these years, her snoring must have become a source of white noise for him. Finally, after an hour or so, Carol came to bed. John laid there, pretending he was already fast asleep to avoid any potential attempt of affectionate behavior from her. Before long, the roaring vibrations in Carol's throat and her struggling gasps for air played the song of a familiar lullaby that let John drift off to sleep, albeit with clenched teeth.

VIII

Chapter 8

As the weeks passed, Carol began to sink deeper into a depression brought on by John's behavior. He started coming home late from work every day, taking off for business trips that he had not had to go on in years, and his callous attitude towards her compounded the desolation she felt.

Desperate for some relief from the anguish, Carol searched for ways to escape the hell she was suffering in. The thought of joining a gym to burn off some nervous energy crossed her mind. She read some research that exercise elevates a person's mood, but it seemed pointless since her dieting had failed yet again. She tried to write a novel, thinking she could create a fantasy world filled with joy and happiness that she could escape to, even if it were only in her mind. However, soon into her writing, she learned that she didn't know those emotions well enough to write about them. Every story that she put pen to paper was as depressing as her own life had become. Carol couldn't even find delight in knitting because she kept focusing on the very situation that she was trying to free her mind from between every stitch. Then it finally came to her. She was going to get a job.

It was the perfect solution to her dilemma. Carol thrived on being needed, and focusing on tasks for someone else seemed to be the answer to her prayers. The only issue to overcome was John's opposition to her working. He never wanted her to hold down a job because he felt it would interfere with her duties around the house. He had always been utterly against it. However, for the first time in her life, she didn't care what John thought. It was something that she had to do for herself. Not for financial independence, but mainly for a sense of self-worth and mental distraction.

Carol slowly started to comprehend that all the years of affection, support, and nurturing she gave John was not because he needed it. It was because she needed to give it to him. The clean home, exquisite meals, perfectly kept yard and garden, clean laundry, all of it was essential for Carol to feel needed and possibly even appreciated. It appeared that the only thing John thought he needed was a young, petite, twenty-something-year-old woman with large breasts, and that was the one thing Carol could not be for him.

Carol realized what a fool she was, having believed that John ever desired her, that she was loved and needed when she was nothing more than a live-in housekeeper to him. It was clear that her entire life was one big lie that she perpetrated herself.

As soon as John walked in the door from a leisurely Sunday afternoon playing golf, Carol told him, "I know you just got home, but I need to tell you something, then I'll leave you alone."

"What is it?" John huffed.

"Tomorrow morning, I am going to start looking for a job."

"I think that would do you some good."

"You do?" Carol asked in disbelief at his agreeable manner.

"Yeah. This funk you've been in makes me depressed. I hate coming home anymore."

"I'll still keep up on the house and make sure the hours don't interfere with having dinner ready for you."

"Don't worry about that. Without any experience, you may have to take whatever you're offered. It'll be fine." John told her. Knowing that if Carol worked odd hours, it would free up even more time to spend with Kayla.

A stunned Carol said, "Thank you for being so understanding."

"No problem. Oh, I will be gone for the week. I leave for Atlanta tomorrow morning for a last-minute business trip. I got the call while I was on the golf course."

"The company sure is sending you on a lot of business trips lately. You haven't been gone this much in years."

"I know, but I can't get out of this one. The company wants me to show the ropes to a new associate and put out a fire that popped up."

"I guess that makes sense to send their best to train someone at fixing all these issues the company seems to be having lately. Hopefully, having someone else available will mean you won't have to take all these out-of-state trips all the time. I'll start my job hunting after I take you to the airport. What time is your flight?"

"That won't be necessary. I have a town car picking me up at eight."

"Okay. I'll get dinner started and let you relax."

Carol combed through the Sunday newspaper and searched the internet for job prospects. She also wrote up her first resume while she was cooking dinner. It seemed almost absurd to write one without having any experience to list, but Carol wanted to come across as professionally as possible. After hours of searching for a job, Carol felt she was qualified for eight of the positions. However, there were only two listed as no experience necessary.

Monday morning, Carol woke even earlier than usual, long before the sun rose, so that she could get ready for her job search. With her hair and makeup flawless and wearing her favorite dress, she felt more confident and beautiful than ever as she prepared John's breakfast.

Once again, Carol shouted up the staircase that John's breakfast was ready, and he came rushing down the stairs with his suitcase in hand.

"Nothing like waiting until the last minute. My ride will be here soon." He said as he sat down at the table.

"Sorry. It took a little longer than I expected to get ready this morning."

"That's right. You're job hunting today. Good luck with that."

"What do you think?" Carol asked as she slid off her apron to get John's opinion if she looked professional enough.

"It tastes fine." He replied between bites of the eggs.

"No. I mean, how do I look?"

Just then, there was a knock at the door, which prompted

John to say, "That's my ride. I need to get going. I'll be back Friday around six in time for dinner."

John grabbed his suitcase and rushed out the door without ever responding to her question or saying goodbye. It was in typical John fashion, especially in these last few weeks for some reason.

Carol stood there in the kitchen for a moment, unsure of what to make of things. Not so much about the business trip he is taking. No, she was confident he's taking another woman on vacation with him, although she couldn't prove it. What had Carol dismayed was her indifference to everything. The business trip, his lack of interest in her, leaving without saying goodbye, everything. It doesn't matter to her anymore. The only thing that did matter was starting a career. With one last check in the hallway mirror, she grabbed her list of jobs and set out to put in applications.

Carol's spirit held up quite well for the first few days of job hunting. She diligently answered every job posting she could find but felt defeated in her effort by Friday morning. All the places she applied at had an excuse as to why she should not be expecting a call for an interview. They were looking for someone with experience, or they were looking for a different type of candidate. What that meant to Carol was someone younger, prettier, and thinner. Out of desperation, Carol called Lisa.

"Hey, Carol! How's your week of freedom from John going?"

"Okay, I guess."

"Just okay?"

"Well, I've been reflecting a lot on myself and my marriage. I have come to some startling revelations."

"Don't tell me. You finally realized that you are too good for John and leaving him. Is that it?" an upbeat Lisa hoped out loud.

"Heaven's no."

"Then what is this epiphany all about?"

"I have realized that I may never get John to change his ways, and no matter how hard I try, I'm never going to be enough for him."

"I'm sorry, hon. I know that must be hard to come to grips with, but remember, it isn't that you're not good enough for him. It's because you are too good for him!"

"Thanks, Lisa."

"If you realize that he will never change, why don't you leave him?"

"It's not quite that simple. I do love John. That's why I married him."

"What are you going to do about it then?"

"Well, I have also realized that I have become too dependent on John emotionally and financially. Because of that, I have decided to get a job to meet some new people and start doing things independently."

"That is a great idea, Carol. Have you thought about what kind of work you would like to do?"

"I'd take anything that is offered to me at this point."

"I'm sure you will find something fantastic once you start looking," Lisa said in support of her best friend.

"That's the problem. I've been looking all week, and I

haven't had any luck at all. Not once has anyone showed interest in hiring me!"

"It takes a little time. Just be patient."

"I'm out of patience. I have been patient with everything in my life. All I want is a job. I would work hard and be a model employee."

"I know you would, Carol. You're a great friend, a phenomenal wife, and would be an asset at any company lucky enough to hire you."

"I'm glad you feel that way. It makes it easier for me to ask a favor from you."

"Anything for you, Carol. Do you need a reference? Some help with a resume? What do you need?"

"I was hoping that you could pull some strings to get me hired at the company you work for."

"I don't think they're hiring right now. Otherwise, I would help you out." Lisa said.

"Please, Lisa. I will take anything! Janitorial, mailroom, secretary, anything."

"I'm sorry, Carol. I can't."

A moment of silence came across the phone before a disappointed Carol said, "I guess I'm on my own then. Out of all the people in my life, you were the one person I thought I could count on for help."

"Carol, it isn't that I don't want to help. I have a rather unconventional job, and I don't think you would want to work where I do."

"I need something, and my options are limited. I'll do anything." a desperate Carol pleaded.

"I think we need to talk about this. Meet me at Caffé

Latte-Da in an hour, and we can discuss what it is that I actually do over a cup of coffee."

"Thanks, Lisa! I knew you'd come through for me."

"Don't get too excited. There's a lot you don't know about my job."

"That's fine. It can't be that bad. I'll see you in an hour."

Carol felt as if the weight of the world had been lifted off her shoulders. Getting a job would bring a much-needed diversion from the mundane day-to-day life of hers. Not to mention making her feel more secure and confident in her abilities.

Although she was only meeting her friend for coffee to discuss the possibility of a job, Carol dressed the part for an actual job interview. Every aspect of her appearance was meticulously groomed and double-checked before she left the house.

When Carol arrived at the coffee shop, Lisa motioned for Carol to join her at her table.

"Look at you. You look incredible! Why are you so dressed up? Have a hot date or something?" Lisa joked.

"I've always heard that you dress for the job you want, not for the job you're applying for when going to an interview. Besides, I didn't think showing up in the house robe and slippers of a homemaker would make a good impression on you nor the clientele of Caffé Latte-Da ." Carol replied with a giggle.

"Well, you made an impression on me. Of course, you're probably way overdressed for anything I can offer you."

"I'll take whatever you have to offer." an anxious Carol blurted out.

"Be careful of what you ask for."

The waiter, a young man in his early twenties, came over to their table and said, "Hi, Lisa. Always a pleasure to see you. Who's your friend?"

"Andrew, this is my friend Carol."

"It's a pleasure to meet you, Andrew," Carol said with an outstretched hand.

"The pleasure is all mine." He said with a smile while politely shaking her hand. "How do you know each other? Do you work together?"

"Not yet, but it is a possibility," Carol replied.

"You will have to let me know if you do start working together. I'd be extremely interested."

"Andrew!" Lisa said sternly. "Get us a couple of cups of coffee and be quiet!"

Andrew sheepishly said, "Yes, ma'am. I apologize." as he shuffled away to get their coffees.

"That was a bit rude, don't you think?" Carol said, questioning Lisa's attitude.

"Look, there isn't an easy way to say this, and I really hope that you don't think less of me after I tell you." Lisa nervously stated.

"Lisa, you can tell me anything. You know I will always regard you in the highest esteem. I love you, girl."

Lisa took a deep breath and paused before saying, "Whew, this is harder than I thought it would be."

"Wait. Are you dating Andrew? Is that what's so hard to tell me?"

"Not exactly," Lisa said.

"Good. There is a bit of an age gap there. Not that there

is anything wrong with that, and you know I'd support you if something was going on." Carol assured her.

"Andrew is a client of mine."

"A client?" Carol asked, not sure what Lisa meant by that statement.

"There's a lot that you don't know about my job."

"Then enlighten me," Carol said.

"I'm a dominatrix," Lisa said while slightly blushing. "Very few people know about this. Honestly, outside of my clientele and a few other ladies in the business, nobody else knows besides you now."

"Let me get this straight. You're telling me that you are a prostitute?" Carol whispered.

"Absolutely not!" Lisa defended herself and her profession. "I don't have sex with any of my clients. People pay me to dominate them. There is a big difference."

Carol was so hyper-focused on what Lisa had told her that she didn't notice Andrew about to set their coffees down on the table when she blurted out, "A dominatrix! You are a dominatrix?"

"The best in the state!" Andrew said, interjecting himself into their private conversation.

"Andrew, will you please go do your job and stay out of this conversation?" Lisa scolded him.

"I'm sorry," Andrew said softly while slowly backing away from the table.

"So, what exactly does a dominatrix do?" Carol inquired.

"People pay me to dominate them. Sometimes it is more of a verbal control type of thing telling them to do humiliating things. Sometimes, it includes spankings, whips, clamps, paddles, and restraints to punish them. Whatever happens varies from person to person. However, it all comes down to taking control of them physically and psychologically."

"And there isn't any sex involved?"

"None," Lisa assured her. "Well, usually, there isn't. There have been a couple of times that I did get excited. One thing led to another, and I did have sex with them, but that's not why they come to me. And, most importantly, that's not what I get paid to do!"

"I don't understand why people would pay someone to do that to them," Carol admitted her oblivious nature to this sort of thing.

"Over the years, I've come to realize that it is like a form of therapy for them. Some people are always in control and held responsible for everything at work and home, so they come to me to relinquish that control for a little while. Others find the pain, punishment, and submission erotic. Then there are those kinky freaks that just can't get off any other way. Those are the ones that have some very severe mommy issues."

"I still don't get it. But it is fascinating, nonetheless." Carol admitted.

"So, do you still want to apply for that job with me?"

"Uh, I don't think I can do that kind of work."

"Neither did I when I first started doing it, but I have to admit that I find it somewhat therapeutic for me too now."

"Really? I still don't think it's for me."

"It generally pays around two hundred dollars an hour."

"What? Are you kidding?"

"Nope. There is a lot of money to be made in this line of

work. Why don't you attend one of my sessions to see what I do and what it's like?"

"I guess that couldn't hurt. Okay, I'll go to one."

"Great! Andrew has an appointment Monday at noon. Would that work for you?" Lisa asked.

"I guess. He is kind of cute for a young guy, but I don't want to get weirded out or anything by spanking him like his mom or something." Carol said cautiously.

"Don't worry. Andrew doesn't have mommy issues. He merely finds aggressive and assertive women attractive. He is harmless, I swear. The other good thing is that since he has already shown interest in you, I know he will pay extra for the session."

"Where is this appointment at?"

"My place. I turned my basement into a dungeon. I had a client that was a contractor, and we exchanged services to get it built. It was completely worth it too!" Lisa told her.

"Interesting. All the times I have been over to your house, I never once thought you had a torture chamber right below my feet. What would a dominatrix wear? Should I bring a negligee with me or what?"

"Wear something comfortable. I'll have something for you to change into when you get to my place."

"This is more than slightly scary for me but exciting too at the same time," Carol admitted before finishing her last sip of coffee.

"I need to pick up a few things for work. Would you like to tag along?"

"Things for work? Do you mean one of those adult bookstores?" Carol asked.

"Of course. I can't get things I need for work at an office supply store."

"I think I'll pass. It's one thing to come to your house for a private appointment, but it's another thing to be spotted at one of those places. What if someone notices me going in there?"

"They would think now there's a fun woman!" Lisa laughed.

"I would be too embarrassed to go in there."

"That's okay. I'm glad we had this talk. Now I can share with you what I do for a living. I'm sorry I lied to you about it for so long, but I didn't want you to think I was a pervert."

"It does sound a little perverted, but if it pays as much as you say it does and there isn't any sex involved, I'll keep an open mind about it," Carol told her.

"I think you will be surprised at how easy it is. You can set your own hours, work as much or as little as you want, as well as make plenty of money doing it." Lisa said while reaching into her purse to pay for the coffee.

"I got it." Carol insisted. "It's the least that I can do for someone who may have found work for me."

"Thanks, Carol."

"Besides, depending on how things go on Monday, you may be buying me cocktails to help erase my memory." Carol laughed.

"It won't be that bad. Thanks again, Carol."

Later that evening, Carol was sitting in the living room when she heard the kitchen side door open.

"John? Is that you?" she called out.

"Who else would it be?" John yelled back.

Carol went to the kitchen to greet John and asked, "How was your trip?"

"It went well."

"Looks like you get quite a bit of sun while you were in Atlanta," Carol said.

"Yeah, we played a fair amount of golf while there. It wasn't that big of an issue to take care of after all, so we had some extra time on our hands."

"That's funny. My weather app said it rained most of the week out there."

John thought for a second and replied, "It was on and off, but not a constant rain. What were you doing checking the weather out there anyway?"

"I was missing you, and it made me feel closer to you. That's all." Carol told him.

"That's weird. Are you sure you weren't checking up on me to try to catch me in a lie? Because that's what it sounds like to me. You don't understand that I work hard to afford all of this crap we have, and sometimes that means I have to be on the road." John said defensively.

"I do trust you, John, as much as I can anyway. You haven't made it easy for me, you know."

"I knew it! As soon as I walk in the door, you start the accusations then wonder why I don't want to spend time at home with you. It's because of your behavior, Carol. Now, since I have told you how my trip was and why I do not want to spend time with you, what's for dinner?"

"I already ate. I wasn't anticipating you wanting dinner, so I picked something up for myself earlier." Carol said.

"I told you when I left that I would be home Friday

evening. You knew I was coming home from the airport. You don't do a damn thing but sulk all day. The least you can do is get off your fat ass and make sure your husband is taken care of!" John shouted at the top of his lungs.

"You've been coming home late for the last four weeks and eating out with your new 'business associate' more than you've been eating at home. I figured you would get something to eat with her, or him, or whoever it is."

"Here we go again with the accusations!"

"No, not at all. I'm only saying that I don't know who this new business associate is." Carol said.

"Sounds like an accusation to me."

"Take it how you want to, John."

"That's it! I need to get out of here and away from your insanity."

"Don't bother. I will leave this time. I need to clear my head." Carol said.

"Go then. Make sure you clear your head entirely of all this crap before you come back because I will not tolerate it any longer."

Carol stormed out to her car, her hands trembling so intensely that she couldn't get the keys in the ignition to start it. Carol tried to focus on a peaceful image in her mind to stave off the anxiety attack she was about to have. Still, the pace of her rapid breathing kept intensifying. Finally, Carol filled her lungs with as much air as she could and let out a blood-curdling scream so loud that it triggered the neighbor's dogs to start barking, but it calmed her enough to get the car started.

Immediately, Carol headed straight to Lisa's house. She needed to talk it out to process everything in her mind and figure out if she is crazy or if John had pushed her over her tolerance limit.

When Carol arrived at Lisa's house, her puffy red eyes made it clear that she was distraught.

"Oh my! What is wrong?" A concerned Lisa asked as she motioned for Carol to come in.

"I think I'm losing my mind."

"Don't be ridiculous. You seemed fine earlier today. Tell me what happened."

"I was okay this morning, but after we had coffee, I had too much free time on my hands and started thinking about John and how he has been acting lately."

"Okay. Well, he has been putting in a lot of hours at work lately."

"Yeah, that's the problem. I don't think John is actually at work the entire time."

"Do you think he's having an affair again?" Lisa asked.

"I don't know what to think. Sometimes this feels all too familiar yet different at the same time. Maybe I'm just paranoid about it."

"You have reason to be worried about it. I'm highly doubtful that you're losing your mind." Lisa assured her. "Is that all? Are you just upset because of your distrust of John?"

"No. When John came home, I did everything shy of coming right out and accusing him of having an affair. Naturally, we got into a huge argument."

"Oh, I see. Maybe the two of you should sit down and talk it out somewhere neutral, so neither of you will get defensive and start yelling." Lisa suggested.

"John doesn't want to talk about it. He would have to care

about me to do that, and he doesn't care anymore. He stopped caring a long time ago." Carol confided.

"Tonight isn't the night to try it, but maybe after a good night of rest, you two can try talking about how you both feel. Do you want to spend the night here?"

"I would like that. I'm afraid if I go home, John will leave. Then I will be up all night wondering where he is."

"Not a problem, hon. You know where the guest room is. Make yourself at home. Do you want something to eat?"

"No, thank you. I think I'm going to lay down. It has been an exhausting week."

"Okay. If you need to talk or start feeling in the dumps again, wake me up, and we can sit up all night talking if you need to."

"Thanks, Lisa. You're the best friend anyone could ask for." Carol said as she hugged Lisa then headed to the guest room.

IX

Chapter 9

Saturday morning, a groggy Carol woke up to the aroma of freshly brewed coffee and stumbled into the kitchen where Lisa was already preparing breakfast for the two of them.

"Hey, sleepyhead." a perky Lisa said.

"Good morning," Carol replied while trying to stifle a big yawn.

"Did you sleep well?"

"I think so. I was out as soon as my head hit the pillow. I don't know how long I slept, but I feel like I could use a couple more hours of sleep."

"Really? You slept for ten hours."

"Are you kidding me? I haven't slept that long in twenty years."

"Here, you probably need this," Lisa said as she handed Carol a cup of coffee. "Are you hungry?"

"Wow! It's strange being pampered like this, but I would love some breakfast."

"What do you mean, pampered? It is only coffee and a frozen waffle. I'm not a gourmet cook like you."

"John hasn't made a single pot of coffee for me, or even for himself for that matter, since we've been together," Carol revealed to Lisa.

"I don't know how you do it." Lisa said in disbelief.

"It's who I am. I'm a caregiver by nature, but I could quickly get accustomed to this."

"I don't want to bring anything up that will upset you, but have you given any thought about what you're going to do about John?"

"I haven't decided yet. Honestly, I'm not looking forward to going back there, let alone having to talk to that man."

"You can stay here as long as you need to. I have the room and love having the company." Lisa said.

"I appreciate that, Lisa. If you don't already have plans, maybe we can go shopping, head to the spa, or go out to dinner tonight. Just have a little fun, you know?"

"My weekend is wide open. Let's do it!" Lisa excitedly said.

"Which would you like to do?" Carol asked.

"Why can't we do it all?" Lisa asked in response.

"I guess we can. It will be a girls' weekend!"

"Absolutely! Let the party begin!"

Carol stayed at Lisa's house the entire weekend. It was the most fun she has had in ages. However, by Sunday evening Carol started to feel a little depressed again.

"What's wrong, Carol?" Lisa asked.

"Nothing is wrong. Why are you asking?"

"I can see it on your face. Something is bothering you. Is there something else you wanted to do this weekend?"

"No. I had so much fun. I couldn't imagine it being any better than it was. I just started thinking about John. It has been forty-eight hours since I stormed out of the house, and he has not called once. I could be lying in a hospital bed, and he wouldn't know it. It demonstrates how much he doesn't care about me. At the least, it show's me that he cares more about whoever he is spending his time with."

"I wish there were something I could do to make it better for you," Lisa responded.

"You have done so much for me already. I don't think I could've made it through this weekend without you."

"The weekend isn't over with yet. Let's get a bowl of ice cream and watch a movie." Lisa suggested.

"It's getting late. I think I better go home. I have to face the music sooner or later."

"Then make it later. You may as well spend tonight here too. You're going to have to come here tomorrow for work anyway. You didn't forget that you're a working stiff now, did you?"

"I kind of did forget." Carol laughed. "You twisted my arm. I'll stay another night."

The following morning as they were eating breakfast, Lisa asked, "Are you ready for your first day at work?"

"I'm not sure, but I have a feeling it will be interesting."

"I'll give you a tour of the dungeon after we finish breakfast."

"That is so creepy to think that you have a dungeon in your basement."

"A girl has to have a place to work." Lisa chuckled.

"I suppose, but is it safe to have these types of people knowing where you live?"

"I have a great clientele and only take on new clients that are referred to me by my current ones. So, I'd say it's pretty safe."

"How did you start doing this? Better yet, why?" Carol asked.

"I started doing this about six years ago. As for the how and why, I suppose for the same reason that you're here. When Robert left me and filed for divorce, I couldn't find employment either. I had bills to pay and, since he and I dabbled with this stuff in the bedroom anyway, it was an easy transition for me to turn it into a career."

"Oh. Well, John and I are not getting a divorce. I'm only trying to find something to occupy my time, make a little spending money, and give me a little more confidence in myself."

"I didn't mean to imply that you and John were splitting up. Just that I couldn't find work either when I first started looking." Lisa explained. "Are you ready for the grand tour?"

"As ready as I'll ever be." Carol sighed.

Lisa led Carol down the creaking basement steps into the dungeon that was dimly illuminated by small slivers of sunlight peeking around the thick drapes covering the windows.

"Don't you have lights down here? I can barely see."

"There are a few, but I wanted you to experience what it is typically like down here. Don't worry. Nothing is going to hurt you. Let your eyes slowly adjust to the darkness." Lisa assured her as she grabbed Carol's arm and guided her across the room.

Suddenly an intensely bright, crackling white light flashed in front of Carol's face.

Carol screamed, "I can't see!" as she pulled away from Lisa's grasp.

"You're fine." Lisa giggled as she pulled open one of the drapes to let in some light revealing Carol crouching down on the dungeon floor with her arms covering her face. "Honey, it's okay. Look. I opened the curtain." Lisa continued saying while trying to pry Carl's arms from her face.

"What the hell was that?" Carol asked.

"It was my stun gun that has an extremely bright strobe light on it to disorient an attacker. I occasionally use it with new clients because once they come in from the direct sunlight, their eyes have difficulty adjusting to the dark, just like yours did. It's somewhat funny because it freaks them out a bit. Plus, it also prolongs their eyes from adapting to the darkness. The longer you can keep them from being able to see, the more intense the session will be since they don't have any idea of what to expect next."

"Kind of freaks them out? It almost made me pee my pants!"

"I'm sorry. I had no idea that it would freak you out that much, but I couldn't resist." Lisa chuckled in response.

"I can't believe people pay you to do stuff like that to them."

"They pay me to do that and a whole lot more," Lisa said with outstretched arms to direct Carol's attention around the room.

Carol stood silently in the middle of the room, slowly pivoting around as she methodically took in this strange new world she found herself in. She recognized a handful of items from her readings about medieval history and some that were common knowledge. Still, for the vast majority of equipment in the dungeon, Carol had no clue about what they were, how to use them, or even why anyone would want to be subjected to such things.

Along the walls hung a plethora of whips in various sizes. A couple resembled small bullwhips. Others had multiple tails of leather emanating from shorter handles and a few with leather balls attached to the ends.

Carol asked in disbelief, "Why do you have so many whips? Are they like stage props or decorations?"

"No, those are tools of the trade."

"Why do you have so many of them? I would assume that just a couple would suffice."

"They may look alike, but I assure you that they couldn't be more different. Each one is made with different kinds of material or shapes to inflict the desired amount of discomfort. For instance, this flogger looks very intimidating with its many tails, but it's constructed out of soft, thin leather. It doesn't sting as much, but it gives an excellent cracking sound when striking someone with it. However, the one next to it is crafted out of thick buffalo hide. It stings like hell."

"I can't wrap my mind around someone wanting to be hurt. All of this is so overwhelming."

"Different stroke for different folks, Carol. That's all it is. Some people have a high pain tolerance. Some want to be brought to tears. Others just want a little erotic play."

"I don't want to hurt anyone, Lisa. That's not who I am."

"They all have a safeword that they will say when things

get too intense. Remember, you're not doing anything they do not want to be done to them. It's like I said before, it's a form of therapy in a roundabout way."

"In the past, electroshock treatments were supposed to be a form of therapy too. That didn't end up being so therapeutic, did it?" Carol rebutted.

"I do that too, in a way," Lisa said as she opened a case on the shelf. "This is called a violet wand. It emits a low watt, high-frequency stream of electric current."

"That must hurt horribly!"

"It depends on the setting and to which body part you apply it. It feels somewhat effervescent on a low setting, much like taking a bath in a tub full of champagne. Turn it up, and it can feel like getting shocked by static electricity or worse! Mostly because the sensation is constant for as long as the wand is in contact with their skin. Do you want to try it?" Lisa asked.

"Hell no!"

"Come on. You should have an idea of what things are going to feel like to be a good dominatrix. I'll put it on the lowest setting."

"It won't hurt?" a nervous Carol asked.

"Not a bit. Here, give me your hand."

Carol hesitantly offered her hand to Lisa.

"Just relax and take in the sensation."

Lisa ran the wand across the back of Carol's hand, up her forearm, to the underside of her upper arm.

"That feels strange but kind of good," Carol admitted.

"Do you want to feel it a little more intense?"

"Sure."

Lisa set the wand to medium intensity and pressed it against the underside of Carol's upper arm.

"Ouch! I thought you said it wasn't going to hurt." Carol shrieked as she yanked her arm away from Lisa.

"You said you wanted to feel it at a higher setting."

"Yeah, but not at the highest setting!"

"That wasn't the highest setting. Honest, it wasn't."

"It felt like I got stung by a bee."

"Now imagine if I set to the highest setting, and you got touched somewhere extremely sensitive like a nipple," Lisa said.

"I'd probably pass out," Carol admitted.

Lisa laughed, "Like I said, different strokes."

"This is so mind-boggling."

"You'll get acquainted with it. Nobody is a pro at it in the beginning. Before you know it, people will be lining up to be disciplined by you."

"Maybe, if I ever get used to this."

"You will. Trust me. After a while, there won't be much that creeps you out. You may not get turned on by it, but it will just be part of the job to you and nothing more." Lisa said.

Carol shook her head in disbelief that anything regarding this kind of lifestyle would ever be normal to her.

"We have about an hour until Andrew gets here for his session, so let's get you ready. I picked up an outfit for you yesterday. It's in my bedroom on the sitting chair."

Carol followed Lisa up the stairs to the normality and safety of her everyday life. At the top of the stairs, Carol paused and peered down into the dark basement dungeon.

"What's wrong?" Lisa asked.

"Nothing. It's just this weird feeling that I have."

"It's all new to you, and you're nervous. It's perfectly normal to have apprehensions. You'll get over it. I promise." Lisa said, trying to be a source of encouragement.

"That's not it. I mean, sure, I'm a little nervous, but standing up here, I feel like there is a part of me that would rather be down there. It's hard to explain."

"Maybe you're a natural at this and just have to get over your anxiety of the first few sessions."

"I doubt that, but we shall see."

When they got to Lisa's bedroom, Carol opened the bag containing her outfit for this afternoon's session.

"Hell no!" Carol exclaimed as she held up a black leather corset.

"This is the outfit of a dominatrix. You'll look gorgeous in it."

"Where's the rest of it?"

Lisa opened another bag on the chair and removed a matching black leather skirt, fishnet stockings, and gloves.

"I also have an extra pair of thigh-high boots you can wear."

"I can't wear this!"

"At least try it on." Lisa pleaded.

"You have to be joking. Seriously, where's the outfit you got for me?"

"This is it." Lisa chuckled.

"No. I'm not going to be wearing that."

"What's the harm in trying it on? We've tried on silly

things at department stores before. I'll put my outfit on too, so you won't be so self-conscious."

"Alright, but no laughing."

"I promise."

Carol went into the bathroom to change into her new outfit. Five minutes later, Lisa knocked on the door and asked, "Do you need some help?"

"Yeah, do you have a long coat I can wear over this?"

"Let me see how you look."

"No way. I'm not coming out of here dressed like this."

"Come on. I have my outfit on."

Carol cracked open the bathroom door and saw Lisa decked out head to toe in a leather miniskirt, thigh-high boots, and a skin-tight blouse with a plunging neckline that showed more cleavage than it concealed.

"You look pretty hot in that outfit. I just look like an exploded can of dough." Carol said.

"Will you stop. I'm sure you look fantastic. Just open the door."

"Fine. But remember, no laughing."

"I won't. Let me see how sexy you look."

As the door opened, a look of wide-eyed surprise on Lisa's face was enough for Carol to try to close the door quickly, but her attempt to conceal herself was unsuccessful as Lisa's foot blocked the door's pathway.

"You look incredible! Better than I pictured you would." Lisa gushed.

"You're crazy. Now move your foot so I can get out of this thing."

"Are you kidding me? That outfit completely suits you. We just need to adjust your hair and makeup to go with it."

"That's hilarious, Lisa. My fat is squishing out between all the gaps in this outfit. Beneath the corset, over top of the boots, and the skirt barely covers the bottom of my huge ass."

"Will you stop bashing yourself. The men will fall in love with you. A tall, full-figured woman brandishing a whip will make them feel even more meager and will solidify you as being the one in charge."

"I don't know. It's one thing to dress up for your lover that you're comfortable with; it's another thing to be seen by strangers like this."

"That's the beauty of it, Carol. They are strangers. They don't know you. You will probably never see them outside of the sessions. Besides that, I know they will be drooling over you and begging you to punish them."

"I don't know how I let you talk me into things, but I will try it one time. Just once!"

"That's all I ask. Now let's do your hair and makeup." A delighted Lisa said.

"What's wrong with my hair and makeup?"

"Nothing. You look wonderful. We just need to put on a thicker coat of war paint."

"I don't want to look any sluttier than I already do." Carol protested.

"I'm not going to make you look like a slut, but you do need to look a bit more aggressive than the soft and subtle look of everyday life. Also, in the low light of the basement, you'll need more makeup on so it will be noticeable."

Lisa applied the perfect amount of makeup on Carol that

left no doubt that she was indeed the vixen in charge before deciding on a hairstyle that would further accentuate her dominant persona.

"Don't pull my hair up in a bun, Lisa."

"Why not? It will keep the hair out of your face so you can see better when you're brandishing a whip."

"Because it's bad enough I look like this as it is! If you pull my hair up, you'll expose the sausage roll on the back of my neck."

"How about a ponytail? Would that be okay?"

"That's fine," Carol said, compromising with Lisa.

Lisa used a little gel to give Carol's hair a wet look and pulled it back in a tight ponytail that would keep her hair out of her face but still gave her an aggressive look.

"There! You are one hot woman!" Lisa said, proud of her work.

"I'm glad the basement is dark," Carol said.

"Enough already. You are a desirable and confident woman."

"I wouldn't use either of those adjectives to describe me, but okay."

While Lisa finished touching up her hair and makeup, Carol nervously paced back and forth in the room.

"Why don't you sit down and relax?" Lisa asked.

"Sit? In this outfit? My ass would probably blow the seam right out of the skirt."

Lisa glanced at her watch, looked out the window, and noticed Andrew coming up the driveway.

"Well, it doesn't matter now. Andrew is right on time. Shake off those nerves, sweetie. It's time to go to work."

X

Chapter 10

Lisa ushered Carol down the basement stairs as Carol's heart began to beat out of her chest, then her hands began to tremble.

Carol said, "I don't think I can do this." at the bottom of the stairs with nervousness in her voice.

Lisa assured her that everything would be fine as she opened a cabinet door revealing a monitor.

"Why do you have a tv down here?" Carol asked.

"It's hooked up to my surveillance cameras. This way, I know who is at the door and if they're alone."

"I thought you said you had great clients and felt safe doing this stuff in your home?"

"I do feel safe, but a girl can't be too cautious," Lisa said as she zoomed the focus in on Andrew.

"Wow. Andrew looks quite different than he did when I met him at his job."

"Sounds like you have a little crush on him," Lisa told her.

"Absolutely not! He is adorable, but I am a married woman, and he is way too young."

"You're married, honey, not dead. It's okay to find other people attractive."

"I don't know about that. The one thing I am curious about is how can Andrew afford your rates on a waiter's paycheck?"

"He's not just a waiter. Andrew is the co-owner of Caffé Latte-Da."

"I can't believe someone like him that is cute and successful would be into this stuff."

"We get all kinds, sweetie."

When Andrew pressed the buzzer to gain access, Lisa barked through an intercom, "Who is it." Although she was fully aware of who it was.

"Your noon appointment, Mistress."

"You may enter. You also know my requirements. Do not anger me by failing to follow directions." Lisa instructed Andrew before pressing the latch release button that allowed him in.

Once inside the six-foot-by-six-foot windowless room lit by an excessively bright fluorescent light, Andrew immediately placed his payment into the drop box located to the right of the dungeon's entrance door.

"Rule number one is always to get the payment first," Lisa told Carol while retrieving the money.

Carol remained fixated on the monitor, watching Andrew undress just on the other side of the door while Lisa counted the money.

Noticing Carol's obvious intrigue of Andrew, Lisa said, "He has a solid muscular build, doesn't he?"

"Yes...he...does. Oh, no!" Carol exclaimed.

"What's wrong?"

"I can't let him see me like this!"

"Will you relax?"

"No. I can't do this. Not with him. I'm too embarrassed. Look at me."

"You look fantastic. Besides, Andrew loves full-figured women. That's why I chose that specific outfit for you. To show off your womanly curves. Trust me, he will desire you and will suffer through anything just to please you." Lisa said, attempting to ease her concerns.

"I'm worried that..." Carol stopped mid-sentence when she noticed on the monitor that Andrew was silently standing at the dungeon's closed entry door in his boxer briefs. "Why is he just standing there?" Carol curiously asked.

"He will stand there for half an hour if I make him."

"Incredible." Carol softly said in disbelief.

"Are you ready?"

"As ready as I can be, I suppose."

"Have your eyes adjusted to the darkness?" Lisa asked.

"Yep."

"Okay, I'm going to kill the lights in his room. When I open the door, we will each grab an arm of his and rush him to the Saint Andrews Cross. Got it?"

"What the hell is that?" Carol asked.

"It's that wooden X along the back wall."

"That's an ironic name for it," Carol said.

"I never thought about it, but I guess it kind of is. Now, when you grab Andrew, get a good grip. He'll be surprised that two people are tugging at him and may instinctively try to pull away."

"Got it. We haven't even started, and although I am nervous as heck, I'm already kind of getting a rush from this." Carol freely admitted.

"It will get even better! Here we go. It's showtime!" Lisa said as she killed the lights in Andrew's room.

Lisa flung open the entrance door, and they grabbed Andrew by his wrists, almost dragging him across the dungeon floor as he stumbled in the darkness.

Once positioned in front of the cross, Lisa shoved him against it and sternly hollered at Carol, "Strap him down." as she pointed to the cuffs at the ends of the wooden beams.

After securing Andrew to the cross, Lisa grabbed a set of noise-canceling headphones off a nearby shelf to place over his ears as he continually tried to focus his eyes on the mysterious second person hidden in the darkness.

"What are the headphones for?" Carol whispered.

"It's okay to speak in a normal tone. The headphones are streaming white noise. Andrew can't hear a single word we say."

"Nice," Carol said approvingly.

"Close your eyes for a second," Lisa told Carol as the bright strobe light flashed unexpectedly in Andrew's face to keep his sight impaired for a little longer.

"Why don't you use a blindfold?" Carol asked inquisitively.

"Sometimes I do, but I like to mix things up. That way, clients don't know what to expect. Besides, I also want his eyes to focus slowly on you. Just when he thinks he will see who else is in the room, his eyes get blinded again. It will frustrate him."

"I'm still unsure if I want him to see me at all. What do we do now?" Carol asked.

"Grab a couple of those riding crops off the wall," Lisa instructed.

Carol rushed to retrieve the crops as if she would suffer punishment if not quick enough and brought back two different crops. One had small, raised rivets protruding from a heart-shaped paddle at the end opposite of the handle. The other had what appeared to be a five-inch piece of a leather belt attached to the end.

"You should use the flat leather crop," Lisa told her. "It's slightly easier to get a sharp snap with it. Did you secure him well?"

"I think so."

Lisa checked her work and said, "Nope." as she tightened the cuffs on Andrew. "You have to get the restraints very snug. Otherwise, they can slip off, and that kind of ruins the experience. They pay to give up total control, so be strong and let them know who is in charge."

"Sorry."

"Don't be sorry. You're learning. Now, smack the inside of his thigh with the crop."

"Like this?" Carol asked as she tentatively tapped Andrew's leg.

"Harder."

Carol swatted his leg with a little more force.

"Again. Harder!" Lisa commanded.

"Is that better?" Carol asked for approval as Andrew's thigh began to quiver.

"Use more wrist when you swing. Like this." Lisa said as she demonstrated the proper technique.

Andrew grimaced in response to Lisa's whipping as a loud crack reverberated through the dungeon.

Carol tried another swing of the crop to his already tender thigh. This time she snapped her wrist right before the crop made contact precisely as instructed.

Andrew's muscles contracted, and his face contorted, but he barely let out a grunt before his legs finally collapsed, causing his wrists to support his entire body weight from the top of the cross.

"Oh my!" Carol gasped as she dropped the crop. "I think I hurt him."

"He's fine," Lisa assured her as she gently tapped Andrew's leg with her crop encouraging him to stand up. "See. Nothing to worry about."

"That freaked me out."

"It's okay. Now pick up the crop and remember not to show weakness, compassion, or concern. Clients are not here to be coddled.

"I'll try."

"I think his eyes are adjusting," Lisa said as she swung the crop in front of Andrew's face but stopping just short of hitting him. "Yep, he flinched."

"Flash the light again! I'm not ready for him to see me." Carol requested.

"Look at that," Lisa said, pointing to a darkened wet spot on Andrew's gray underwear and tapping the growing bulge contained within with her crop. "It appears he likes your touch as well as how you look." Lisa giggled.

Carol's blushing was instantly discernable even in the dark confines of the dungeon.

"You want Mistress Carol, don't you slave?" Lisa asked as she removed the headphones covering Andrew's ears.

"Yes, Mistress," Andrew replied.

Lisa quickly landed a striking blow from her crop across his chest and asked, "Are you allowed to want anything, slave?"

"No, Mistress."

Another smack of the crop landed across his chest before Lisa asked, "Then why did you say you wanted Mistress Carol?"

"Because she is beautiful, Mistress," Andrew confessed.

"Yes, she is," Lisa said as she pressed the handle of her crop under his chin. "But why would she want anything to do with a waste of human flesh like you?"

"I would do anything for her. Anything!"

"Let's test that statement. Release the slave from the cuffs." Lisa commanded Carol.

Once released from his bindings, Lisa ordered him to his knees, from where he studied every voluptuous curve on Carol.

"Bow down at Mistress Carol's feet!"

Andrew crawled to Carol on his hands and knees and stared at her boots.

Lisa stormed over to the wall and grabbed a wooden paddle. When she returned to her position behind Andrew, she said, "I am severely disappointed in you, slave. You cannot follow the most uncomplicated directions. I told you to bow down at her feet, not stare at them! Ass in the air, forehead on the floor!"

As soon as Andrew obeyed, Lisa swung the paddle and landed two crushing smacks to each side of his buttocks as Carol grimaced with empathy for Andrew.

"That's for your inability to follow orders."

"Yes, Mistress," Andrew grunted.

"Now clean Mistress Carol's boots."

Without hesitation and out of fear of retribution, Andrew wiped off the few specks of dust that were on Carol's boots with his hands.

"I told you to clean her boots! Why are you using your filthy hands?" Lisa shouted at him.

"Because I didn't know what else to use, Mistress."

Lisa grabbed a handful of Andrew's hair and yanked his head back as she shouted in his face, "Use your tongue, maggot!"

Andrew began fervently licking Carol's boot from toe to heel before making his way up the long length of black leather that ended halfway up her thigh. At this point, Andrew paused and inhaled deeply through his nose, hoping to catch the possible vague scent of her femininity mere inches from his face.

Carol, feeling extremely uncomfortable having another man's face so close to an area she had only shared with her husband, took a quick step back.

"Look at what you did, slave. You made Mistress Carol uncomfortable!"

"I am sorry, Mistress Carol. Please forgive me for my disrespectful actions."

"It's okay. I haven't..."

"Quiet!" Lisa yelled, cutting off Carol. "It is not okay. He must be punished for his unacceptable behavior. Now go over there and face the wall, slave." Lisa ordered Andrew.

Andrew stood before the cinderblock wall with his head hanging down in apprehension of the unknown punishment that awaited him for his transgressions as Lisa lead Carol to the wall of whips on the other side of the room.

"Pick one," Lisa told Carol.

"I can't remember which one is the least painful."

"It doesn't matter. Just pick one."

Carol chose a red whip with a dozen tassels hanging from a braided handle.

"Good choice," Lisa said as she grabbed a wooden cane.

"Now, to ensure both of you understand that I am the one who is in charge in this dungeon, you, slave, will put your hands on the wall as Mistress Carol gives you ten lashes with her whip. If you take your hands off the wall, the count returns to zero. Do you understand, slave?

"Yes, Mistress."

"Mistress Carol, if you do not whip him hard enough, I will swat him with this switch, and you don't like that, do you slave?"

"That is correct, Mistress."

"Let the punishment commence!"

Carol stood behind Andrew, twirling the whip around, trying to get a feel for its weight and how hard she should swing it. She didn't want to hurt him, but Carol knew Lisa would significantly elevate Andrew's level of discomfort if it were not enough.

Carol's first swing landed with a pleasant thud, but Andrew barely flinched.

"I'll count that, but you better swing harder!"

Carol swung with more force on the second lashing, causing Andrew's hands to slide down the wall and his back arch in response to the agonizing bite of her whip.

Carol covered her mouth with her hand and looked at Lisa in horror, thinking she inflicted too hard of a hit.

Lisa gave her a nod of approval and asked Andrew, "How many is that, slave?"

"Two, Mistress."

"Again!" Lisa commanded.

Being apprehensive, Carol took a much softer swing for the third lash, which was immediately followed up by a blow from Lisa's cane. Andrew's hands nearly came off the wall, with only his fingertips remaining in contact as he let out a small yelp.

"Do you know why he got hit with my cane?" Lisa asked Carol.

"Because I didn't punish him properly."

"You are learning quickly. Continue!"

Carol took another swing that barely met Lisa's satisfaction.

"Slave, you don't want to feel the sting of my cane again, do you?"

"I would prefer not Mistress."

"Then what do you say to Mistress Carol?"

"Harder, please, Mistress Carol," Andrew begged to avoid another blow from Lisa's cane.

After every swing of the whip, Andrew continued to plead for a harder smack, and Carol obliged.

By the ninth lash, Andrew's back and buttocks were covered with red welts proving that Carol showed little mercy to him as endorphins coursed through his veins, causing his legs to begin quivering. Carol's compassionate nature showed as she pointed it out, but Lisa callously shrugged her shoulders.

"This is the last one. Make it count, Mistress Carol! Are you ready, slave?"

"Yes, Mistress," Andrew said while breathing heavily.

Carol tried to take a little speed off her swing so it wouldn't hurt as bad. She could tell Andrew was at his limit of what he could endure. However, the final lash of Carol's whip failed to meet Lisa's approval.

"No!" Lisa shouted as she forcefully swung her cane against Andrew's buttocks.

For a split second, Andrew's hands came off the wall, but he quickly realized his error and placed them back.

"Did you just remove your hands from the wall?" Lisa asked.

"I'm sorry, Mistress."

"I guess we are back at zero for the count," Lisa said.

"Please, Mistress," Andrew begged for mercy.

"Please what?"

"I have learned my lesson, Mistress. I am sorry."

"Sorry for what, slave? That the count has returned to zero?"

"I am sorry for disrespecting Mistress Carol and for disobeying your order to keep my hands on the wall."

"I'm not sure you have learned your lesson. What do you think, Mistress Carol?"

Carol stood in awe over the transformation that took place before her eyes. The strong, masculine man that entered the dungeon with a slightly perverted side was now a whimpering coward begging for mercy.

"Mistress Carol?" Lisa asked. "Do you feel that he has learned his lesson?"

"I think he has," Carol confirmed.

"Thank you, Mistress Carol. I am extremely sorry for my disrespectful actions towards you."

"Go get dressed, slave. Your session is over with." Lisa said as she opened the exit door.

As Andrew hurried towards the open door, Lisa quickly swung the cane through the air behind him. The all too familiar swooshing sound that meant immediate discomfort caused Andrew to leap through the doorway to safety from Lisa's wrath.

With an evil giggle, Lisa said, "You're pathetic."

"Yes, Mistress," a humbled Andrew replied.

Lisa closed the door and turned on the hidden monitor before asking Carol, "So, what did you think?"

"To be honest, I don't know what to think."

"I suppose it can be a bit overwhelming to experience a slightly more intense session for your first time."

"That's part of it, I guess. I mean, I'm not sure I like hurting people," Carol admitted.

"Again, Carol, you're not doing anything that they don't want."

"I know, but I can't seem to wrap my mind around why they want it."

"Maybe their mommies didn't spank them enough, or possibly they were spanked too much. They may just be twisted freaks. Who cares why they want it? It isn't for us to figure out why." Lisa said as the buzzer rang.

"Another appointment?" Carol asked.

"No, it's Andrew. He's ready to be let out. What is the other part that you're having troubles processing about this line of work?" Lisa asked as she pressed the button to let Andrew out.

"I'm shocked how Andrew seemed to change so drastically. When I saw him on the monitor, he appeared confident and in charge. Then Andrew seemed like a typical pervert during the session when he got slightly aroused. But by the end of everything, he was so meek and timid. Nothing like who he was when he walked in. I wish I could have that effect on John." Carol confessed.

"Maybe we should kidnap John and whip his ass into submission." Lisa joked as she opened the strongbox again. "Oh, look. Andrew left us a tip."

"That's what I mean. Who not only pays to have pain inflicted on themselves and made to feel worthless but also tips?" Carol said as Lisa counted the tip money.

"Who cares?" Lisa said as she handed Carol half of the money collected for the session.

Carol quickly counted the money and exclaimed, "two hundred dollars for an hour of abuse!"

"For Andrew, it is three hundred dollars an hour plus tip. I don't always get that much. It depends on the client. Some only get charged one hundred fifty dollars. But Andrew makes a lot, so he spends a lot. Once you build a rapport with a client, they will pay whatever they can to keep their appointments."

"That's incredible!"

"So now you know how I can afford my lifestyle. Do you want to come back and try it again tomorrow?"

"I'll get back to you on that. There's so much to think about, but right now, I need to change clothes, get this whorish makeup off me, and get some housework done before John gets home."

XI

Chapter 11

Back in her usual attire and the safe confines of her home, Carol started to chip away at her list of chores. Immediately she began to realize that something was different. The contentment Carol once got from cleaning seemed to vanish, and she began to wonder why it was so important to have a perfectly kept home when her life was anything but perfect. Carol questioned everything she had been doing throughout the years and tried to analyze why she did it. Was she trying to make John happy, or was she trying to hide the embarrassment John caused her from the outside world?

Maybe the entire line of thinking was because she made some money today and realizes that she can be more than a simple domestic servant to an unappreciative husband. Yet somehow, she didn't think going to a job as a secretary would make her question her life to this extent regardless of how much she would or wouldn't make.

Her thoughts soon turned to Andrew and how much it appeared that he did desire her. How he even made her feel somewhat sexy in the ridiculous outfit Lisa had picked out for her to wear. There wasn't a single doubt in Carol's head that Andrew would probably do anything and everything for her. That kind of attention was nice, but she wants John. Even when Carol was younger, far thinner than her current stature, and could get any man she desired, John was the only man for her, and she still feels that way. So, the cause of her questioning her life wasn't because of Andrew either.

It had to be the strange new world Lisa introduced into her life. A world where she was in charge and desired. For the first time in Carol's life, she controlled the amount of pain or pleasure someone got rather than being on the receiving end of what someone else was willing to give her. But that's just a fantasy world artificially created and was far from reality. As Carol sat on the couch and scanned the living room, it became evident her home life was a delusional world too. Everything appeared ideal to the outside world, but the truth was that her life and marriage were a complete mess. The Utopian display of a happy home was nothing more than a false representation of reality. It was a fantasy. A fantasy that was quickly dying.

It was then that Carol decided to seek refuge in this new life that presented itself to her. Without hesitation, Carol picked up the phone and called Lisa to accept more training.

"What's up, girl?" Lisa asked.

"What time do I need to come over tomorrow?"

"The next appointment is at one if that's what you're referring to."

"Okay. I'll be over around noon then. Will that work?"

"Sure. What made you decide to give it another shot?"

"Let's just say that I found it very empowering."

"It is that." Lisa agreed.

"Can we go shopping afterward for a couple more outfits?" Carol asked.

"You really did enjoy it, didn't you?"

"More than you know, Lisa."

"I'll see you tomorrow then."

"Bye, Lisa," Carol said with newfound confidence.

As soon as Carol hung up the phone, John walked in the door.

"Oh, you're home," John said.

"Why wouldn't I be?" Carol asked.

"The way you stormed out of here Friday night made me think that you wouldn't be back for a while, especially since I didn't hear from you all weekend."

"I needed some space to clear my head, but I feel much better now. I'll get something started for dinner," Carol replied.

"Don't worry about it. I didn't know if you were going to be here, so I made dinner plans."

"Okay. I'll get my purse and go with you. It'll be a nice treat not to have to cook tonight since today was my first day at work."

"Actually, Carol, I made dinner plans for me, not for us."

"Where are you going?" Carol asked.

"Does it matter?"

"I suppose it doesn't. I was merely curious. Who are you going with?"

"Again, does it matter?" John snapped at her.

"Yes, it does matter. It matters a lot, John!" Carol replied.

"A friend."

"Does this friend have a name?"

"What is with all these questions? Did I grill you about your weekend? Do you know what your problem is, Carol? You need to learn to trust me. I'm not this evil person you make me out to be!"

"I have my reasons not to trust you, John. You know that!"

"So, I messed up a couple of times. It happens. Nobody is perfect."

"A couple of times, John? A couple?"

"You want me to answer your questions? Fine! Yes, my friend has a name. No, I am not going to tell you what it is. I told you I was going out to eat, and no, I'm not going to tell you where I'm going, what I'm eating, or what time I will be home. If that's not good enough, deal with it!" John yelled at the top of his lungs as he stomped out of the house and slammed the door.

Usually, John's callousness would have reduced Carol to a sobering mess, but not a single tear formed in her eyes. Instead, anger raged in her mind, and hatred filled her heart towards the man she vowed to love forever seventeen long and occasionally arduous years ago.

Carol grabbed the closest thing to her, a crystal candy bowl, and hurled it across the room. It and the lamp it hit shattered into thousands of pieces, reminiscent of how destroyed her life, heart, and soul has become.

After John's last known affair, Carol secretly downloaded a GPS tracking app on John's phone. She never used it before because she genuinely did want to believe him, and she hated the thought of being a typical untrusting scorned woman.

However, she had to know if John was having dinner with a friend or seeking comfort in another woman's arms.

Carol opened the app on her phone, and it showed that John was driving north on I-110 towards Los Angeles, but where he was going was still a mystery.

For the next hour, Carol tried to vindicate John in her head, and at one point, she almost had herself convinced that what she was doing was completely unacceptable. However, she was growing weary of always being the willing victim of John's infidelity. So, she opened the app one more time, and it showed that John had stopped in a residential neighborhood of Pasadena for the last fifteen minutes.

As Carol ran through the list of John's know friends and acquaintances in her head, she couldn't come up with a single person that lived in that area. But that alone is not enough to prove that he was with another woman.

All of the thoughts and worries began to take their toll on Carol by emotionally draining her. After a while, she decided that it would be best to put it out of her mind for the rest of the night so, Carol made a little snack and watched a movie in bed, during which she promptly fell asleep.

When Carol awoke in the morning, she yawned and stretched as a smile began to form on her face. However, her typical sunny morning disposition dissipated fast as she realized that she was alone in bed.

"That man had better fallen asleep in his chair," Carol grumbled to herself as she slipped on her robe.

Every step down the staircase came with an increasing amount of suspense regarding what she may find, let alone the tension of how she will react. If John wasn't home, would she confront him when he returned? Leave him? Learn to accept the situation that it is who John is and that he won't change? All these questions filled her mind with anxiety.

When she reached the bottom of the stairs, she slowly peeked around the corner of the wall and saw John sleeping in his recliner. That sight alone should have been enough to put to rest the questions that flooded her mind while coming down the stairs, but they were persistently still haunting her.

Carol sat at the kitchen table, reflecting on the situation while waiting for the coffee to brew. The only thing she kept thinking about was how big of an ass John was. That is until the beeps of the coffee maker distracted her from the negative thoughts.

Carol poured herself a cup of coffee, added a teaspoon of sugar, and began to stir. She stared hypnotically at the funnel starting to form in the center of the coffee as she stirred faster and faster. Carol thought it was ironic how it mirrored her life. It was as if John was the spoon stirring around the blackness of her emotions and sending them spiraling down into an even darker and seemingly endless abyss.

"What's for breakfast?" John asked as he walked into the kitchen. "I'm starving."

"Nothing!" Carol answered boldly.

"What do you mean nothing?"

"I didn't know if you were going to be home or not, so I made plans to go out for breakfast."

John sarcastically chuckled, "That's really funny, Carol."

"It's not a joke. I am going out for breakfast."

"Whatever. Just lose the attitude before I get home for dinner."

"Attitude? You mean my confidence." Carol corrected him.

"Is that what you call it?" John asked.

"Oh, about dinner, I have plans with Lisa after work. So, you will be on your own for dinner too."

"Let me make this as clear as I can for you. Just because you have a little job now, it doesn't negate your duties around this house. You are my wife, and you need to act accordingly." John sternly told Carol.

"Then you need to remember that you are my husband, and when you start acting like it, I will start treating you like it." Carol shot back.

"I don't act like your husband?" John yelled. "Look around you! Ninety percent of the stuff in this house I bought for you. Not for me, Carol. For you! I take damn good care of you."

"Yes, John. You are an excellent provider, but there is more to being a husband than merely taking care of someone financially. I need to feel loved, appreciated, and desired. I want to be touched and made love to."

"Here we go again. I have to get ready for work." John said as he headed upstairs.

An angered Carol opened the app on her phone to find out exactly what John had been up to last night. It may not give any details about what he was doing or with who, but it did show that he was at a specific address for over four hours before coming home.

With a growing animosity towards John, Carol called Lisa.

"Yeah?" a groggy Lisa answered the phone.

"Good, you're up."

"I am now."

"I'm sorry. I didn't realize the time. Go back to sleep."

"It's fine. What's wrong?" Lisa asked.

"That husband of mine infuriates me! Do you want to get breakfast? My treat."

"Uh, sure."

"Great! Get dressed. I'll be right over." Carol said, immediately hanging up the phone without allowing Lisa to negotiate a later arrival time.

Thirty minutes later, Carol honked her car's horn in Lisa's driveway, signaling that she was waiting for her. Carol honked again one minute later, but to a woman in a hurry, it seemed like ten minutes had passed.

When Lisa got in the car, she asked, "Dang, girl. I know you're upset at John, but what is your hurry?"

"I'm sorry. I guess I just have a lot on my mind."

Carol drove down the road and passed several restaurants before turning onto the highway, causing Lisa to ask, "Where are we going?"

"I need to run an errand first. Don't worry. We will still get breakfast."

Lisa nodded off on the drive, which was a good thing since she probably wouldn't have been thrilled to travel ninety minutes during rush hour traffic to Pasadena on an empty stomach.

Carol pulled into the drive-thru of a fast-food restaurant and woke Lisa up by asking, "Okay. What do you want?"

"Where are we?"

"In Pasadena. What do you want to eat?"

"Are you serious? Why did you drive to Pasadena to eat here? We could've gone to the one ten minutes from my house?"

"I'm sorry, Lisa. I'll make it up to you by buying dinner after we go shopping this evening."

Lisa raised her eyebrow in a silent questioning fashion.

"Yes, at a real restaurant," Carol answered her. "What do you want for now?"

"A large cup of coffee. A huge cup of coffee. Heck, see if they will give us the whole pot."

After getting their coffee, Carol continued driving down a couple more side streets before coming to a stop in front of the house that John was at last night.

As Carol intensely stared at the house, Lisa asked, "Can you tell me why we drove to Pasadena to have drive-thru coffee in your car in a residential neighborhood?"

"John spent four hours here last night."

"I see."

"I have to know if he was visiting a friend or with a home-wrecking tramp."

"Well, are you going to knock on the door and see or what?" Lisa asked.

"Heavens no. I don't want John to know I was spying on him if it turns out to be a friend. He'd be so mad I don't know what he would do."

"Do you want me to go to the door?" Lisa offered.

"No. Let's just sit here for a bit and see if anyone comes out."

After an hour passed by without any noticeable activity taking place, Lisa asked, "Do you even know if anyone is home?"

"No. But there is a car in the driveway."

"Well, I need to go to the bathroom."

"So do I. I guess coffee on a stakeout wasn't such a good idea. Can you hold it for another hour? I'd hate to come all this way to go home empty-handed."

"I'll try, but I can't promise anything."

Forty minutes later, while Lisa read the news on her phone, Carol smacked her repeatedly on the shoulder with excitement saying, "We have movement!"

Lisa looked up in time to see the screen door open and a cat stepping onto the porch, but then the door promptly closed without anybody coming outside.

"I didn't see anyone. Did you?" Lisa asked.

"No." A disappointed Carol said with her eyes still fixated on the front door of the house.

"I think we should wrap this up. I really need to pee."

"I guess I'll come back another day," Carol said as she started the car.

Just then, the screen door opened a second time. That's when Kayla stepped out and danced her way to the car in an obviously good mood.

"That S-O-B!" Carol shouted.

"Hold on a sec. We don't know if John was with her. She might be the wife or girlfriend of his friend. Hell, look at her. She's young enough to be the daughter of one of his friends." Lisa said, playing devil's advocate.

"True, but I can tell just by the way she looks. She's precisely John's type. Young, thin, and pretty. I know that asshole screwed her. I just know it!" Carol screamed while pounding her fists on the steering wheel.

"Damning evidence, yes, but it is still not proof."

"Let's follow her," Carol suggested as she put the car in drive.

"Whoa, wait a minute. We don't know much right now. I admit it doesn't look good, but we have an appointment to get ready for and need to go home."

Carol let out a deep sigh. "You're right. But I'm not going to let this go. I will get to the bottom of it! Besides, beating the hell out of someone right about now will help blow off some steam."

"That's not what we do, Carol. It's not only about inflicting pain."

"I know, but it's like you said, it is a form of therapy. You have to admit that it can be as therapeutic for the dominatrix as it is for the sub." Carol argued.

"I'll give you that. Now let's find a bathroom and go home."

Lisa tried having a conversation with Carol on the ride home, but Carol's mind was so preoccupied with whether John was having an affair with that young woman she saw that she only heard half of what was said.

Not much was said while getting ready for their session either until Lisa tried to redirect Carol's attention by saying, "I need you to focus on the job now."

"I am focused."

"You're focused on the wrong stuff. I need your full attention because Dominic isn't like Andrew. He doesn't want to be whipped and spanked. With Dominic, it's about mind control and humiliation."

"I can't even swat him with a crop?" Carol asked.

"No."

"Then how does he get punished for not following commands?"

"We can put him in the dog crate or tie him to the rack and tickle him with a feather."

"Really? That's it?"

"Everyone is different. You must learn all about each submissive and what their limitations and desires are. Some will want extreme punishment and pain, while others can only handle a playful session." Lisa explained.

"That's not what I was expecting," Carol said.

"You have to remove your emotions from this. It is a job and a service that you provide. Maybe you should only observe the session today."

"I'm fine, Lisa."

"I don't think you are. So just watch and learn."

Throughout the session, Carol tried her best to learn about mental domination. However, she was too submissive to her own mind as it kept wondering about that mysterious woman and what connection she had to John.

When the session ended, Lisa told Carol, "It's a good thing you're not getting graded. You would have got a D at best."

"I'm sorry. I can't seem to stop thinking about that woman."

"I understand. Let's try to get your mind off things by going shopping and having dinner. You do owe me dinner, you know."

Lisa finally managed to distract Carol's mind, and they had a splendid day together. However, it was short-lived because Carol eventually had to go home.

When she arrived home, she was pleasantly surprised to

see that John wasn't there. Carol needed proof of John's infidelity before she can confidently confront him about the possible affair. Although she wanted to recheck the app to see what John was up to, Carol figured a good night's sleep would be best rather than stressing out by knowing that he is where she thought he was.

XII

Chapter 12

Over the next several months, Carol became quite skilled at her new profession and made quite the name for herself within the BDSM community. She steadily grew both her clientele and income as she continued working out of Lisa's basement dungeon. However, her favorite client was Andrew. Her affinity towards him had to do with the fact that he reminded her of John when he was younger, which Carol found satisfying when she took her frustrations out on him.

During this time, John and Carol learned to cohabitate together without the endless arguments that were commonplace in their marriage. She still had not earned John's love and devotion, which continued to break her heart, but Carol also didn't have to live with the mental anguish she was once burdened with thanks to Andrew.

For John, nothing mattered more to him than to make Kayla happy. He quickly fell head over heels in love with everything about her. He loved Kayla's energy, bright demeanor, her perfect little body, and he even enjoyed her cooking. She wasn't quite the gourmet cook Carol was, but it satisfied him enough. And the sex was sensational! She did things that no other woman had ever done with him. John couldn't find a single flaw with Kayla. She was everything he had ever desired and more.

Even though Carol was able to cope with John's extramarital activities, one aspect troubled her. Carol could not figure out why John continued to carry on with this particular woman. All of the others in the past had been a one or two time affair to Carol's knowledge. However, John has been seeing Kayla steadily for months now. So, when Carol wasn't working, she was stalking Kayla to learn what had John so fascinated with her. Carol was obsessed with her and studied Kayla's every move, including where Kayla went, her wardrobe, her hairstyle, how Kayla interacted with John, everything. In time Carol felt she knew Kayla better than John did.

Carol eventually had saved enough money to lease an old mom-and-pop restaurant that had closed long ago. It was an ideal location for her dungeon since it wasn't heavily traveled by or have another structure close to it. The building's rehab didn't cost much other than needing a new roof, so most of the finances went towards decorations, soundproofing, and a security system.

Within a month, Carol was able to fill it with the equipment that she collected over the short time she had been a dominatrix and some that Lisa had given to her. It looked nondescript from the outside, but that's what she desired to avoid unwanted attention to such a business. On the inside, the dungeon was majestic. A purple and gold color scheme with slightly brighter lighting than usual may have been a slight deviation from a traditional torture chamber, but it suited Carol. She wanted to be worshipped like a queen more than feared like a shrew. The best part for Carol is that the building was large enough to continue growing her business and to have two or three sessions booked simultaneously, essentially doubling her income.

After putting the finishing touches on her dungeon, a proud Carol called Lisa saying, "I'm ready to open for business!"

"That's awesome! When can you show it to me?"

"Today if you want to. I'll pick you up."

"Come on over. I can't wait!" Lisa said.

Carol was so excited to show off her crown achievement to her best friend that she didn't hesitate a second after hanging up the phone to pick her up.

On the drive back to Carol's dungeon, Lisa said, "I don't know why you've been so secretive about this place. I am dying to see it!"

"It was something I had to do for myself. I had to make it exactly as I had envisioned it. Don't get me wrong, I loved working out of your place, but this is one hundred percent me. I can't wait for you to see it."

"How far is it?" Lisa asked.

"We're almost there," Carol said as she got ready to turn into the driveway.

"What are we doing at this dump?" Lisa asked.

"This is it!" Carol exclaimed. "This is my dungeon or, as you say, my office."

"This place has been closed for years. I'm happy that you

are trying so hard, but you could have done better than this. It looks like it will cost a fortune to fix up."

"That's the beauty of it. It's structurally sound! I had a new roof put on, but the owners took the cost of it off my yearly lease payments. It worked out for both of us that way and lowered the monthly payments down so I could afford to pay three months in advance, which was a requirement since I didn't have much credit history."

"Still, there had to be other options available elsewhere," Lisa said.

"There wasn't very much to choose from, but I think this location is perfect. Just wait until you see the inside." Carol said as she opened the back door. "This is where my clients will come in so that nobody will see their cars from the road."

"Good idea," Lisa said as they walked into the ten-foot by ten-foot changing room.

There was a slot in the wall to deposit payments into the strongbox, three lockers for personal belongings, and a wooden folding chair in the room's center. Other than that, the only decoration was a twenty-foot bullwhip hanging on the wall.

Carol opened the second door that led to the dungeon, saying, "This is my office."

"Wow! This place is beautiful." Lisa said in approval. "You have surpassed everything I could have imagined."

"Thank you. I love it too!" Carol gushed.

"You have much more equipment than I thought you had. A massage table, kneeling bench, dog cages, and I believe you have more whips, paddles, and floggers than I do."

"I even have a couple of overhead pulleys." Carol pointed out.

"You have everything a working girl needs."

"Plus, since this is the old kitchen area, there's even a drain in the floor for easy cleanup."

"You have thought about everything."

"This is my favorite thing about the dungeon," Carol said while leading Lisa to the back wall.

"You have a throne too? Hail to the queen." Lisa laughed.

"Exactly! From here, I can watch all of my submissive pets suffer and be worshiped at the same time if I want to."

"You have come a long way in a short time, my lady," Lisa said while curtsying towards Carol.

"What can I say. I had a great mentor."

"That's true," Lisa said as they both giggled.

"Seriously, I wouldn't be this strong if it weren't for you. I would still be crying myself to sleep and blaming myself for every affair John had."

"You've always been a tough woman. I don't know anyone else that could have handled what you have been through in your marriage. You only needed a little encouragement and a nudge in the right direction for you to see it for yourself."

"Thank you, Lisa."

"I didn't want to pry, so I haven't asked, but how are you and John doing?"

"Not all that well. He's still seeing that whore from Pasadena, but I'm not going to give up without a fight."

"That's the spirit. What's your plan?"

"I don't know, but I need to find a way to stop the heartache. I'm barely holding on by a thread." Carol admitted.

"I wish I had the answer for you, but you will figure it out."

"There is one thing you may be able to answer for me," Carol said.

"What is that?"

"Well, this morning, I received an application from a potential client, and I'm not sure if I should accept it or not."

"If you think they're sketchy, go with your gut feeling and reject it," Lisa told Carol.

"That's not the issue. Everything seems to be fine. Every question was answered fully and with correct spelling too."

"Then what is the problem?"

"It's a woman. I don't know if I can dominate a female submissive."

"You have to remove gender from the equation. A submissive is neither man nor woman. They are simply a submissive. Besides, it's not like you are having sex with her."

"Have you ever dominated a woman?" Carol asked.

"A couple of times, but it isn't really to my liking."

"That's my issue. I don't think I'd like it either."

"You won't know for sure unless you give it a try," Lisa said.

"True, but what if I do try it, and ten minutes into the session, I realize that I hate it?"

"Then make it all about the money. Shoot her a high price. If she agrees to it, concentrate on the money. If you didn't like it, don't book another appointment."

"I suppose I could do that. You always give the best advice." Carol told Lisa.

"Not always, but I try. You better get me back home. I have to get ready for a date."

"You are going on a date? I don't think you have been on a date in a year."

"Yeah, it has been about that long." Lisa agreed.

"Is he into the lifestyle as well?"

"I hope not! It would be too much like work every time we fooled around."

"You have a point. Let's get going."

Carol dropped Lisa off at home and headed back to her dungeon to ensure that everything was ready for her first appointment tomorrow. Upon returning, she promptly sent an email to the new applicant before she could talk herself out of it. Carol explained that since she already has a full stable of submissives that her rate would be three hundred fifty dollars for a non-private session and five hundred dollars for a private session. To Carol's surprise, a reply was immediately sent back, agreeing to a non-private session.

In a way, Carol was disappointed that the woman still wanted to schedule an appointment even with the price being double what her usual rates were. However, she focused on the extra money just as Lisa told her to do, which eased her mind. So, Carol booked the session for two o'clock Friday afternoon.

With a full schedule of clients and other dominatrices wanting a tour of her new workspace, the next few days were hectic. Carol appreciated the attention, but it was exhausting both mentally and physically, especially after all the work it took preparing the new location. The upside to being this busy was that it did help her lose fifteen pounds of excess weight over the last couple of weeks, which bolstered her confidence. It also helped keep hope alive that she can get John to find her desirable again. Everything seemed to be going according to Carol's plan.

Thursday evening, everything changed when someone knocked on the front door of Carol's home.

"Can I help you?" Carol asked the young man at the door.

"Hi, Mrs. Duvall. I don't know if you remember me. My name is Mark. I was at your Christmas party last year."

"Oh, yes. You're Lisa's daughter's boyfriend."

"Belle and I broke up a while ago."

"I'm sorry to hear that. What can I do for you, Mark?" Carol asked.

"It isn't any of my business, but your husband has been dating my friend Kayla for a while."

"You are correct, Mark. It's none of your business." An angry Carol snapped at him. "I am fully aware of my philandering husband's activities."

"I thought you should know that he asked Kayla to marry him, and she said yes."

Carol stood silently at the door with a blank stare on her face.

"Mrs. Duvall. Are you okay?" Mark asked.

"I don't believe a word of this. John, while not the most faithful husband, would never do that!"

"I didn't want to tell you about it, but I swear it is the truth. He's even taking Kayla to Jamaica for a week to celebrate their engagement. They leave Monday morning."

"Is that so?" Carol questioned him.

"I would've told you sooner what was going on, but I didn't recognize Mr. Duvall at first. I knew he looked familiar, but when I figured out who he was and what was happening, I knew I had to tell you."

"I know it wasn't an easy thing for you to do, but I appreciate that you did. I have a lot to think about, so I hope you don't think I'm rude, but..."

"It's fine. I understand and have to be going anyway. I'm sorry, Mrs. Duvall."

Not knowing what to do, Carol went upstairs to her bedroom to think about how she should handle the situation. Burning down the house with everything in it was tempting, but it wouldn't hit him hard enough since everything was insured and replaceable. No, she had to think of something much bigger. The thought of beating him to the punch by getting a high-powered attorney crossed her mind. Then she could take half of everything they own and make him pay alimony since she is technically an unemployed housewife. Her career as a dominatrix was a cash business, so there weren't any reported earnings that she had. Doing that would take some of his money, making it harder for John to spoil that homewrecker of his. Again, that wasn't enough for the hell he has put her through. Carol felt the only proper retribution for giving up half of her life to John was for John to give up half of his life to her.

Carol stayed up the entire night reflecting on her life and trying to devise a plan of attack, but she still didn't know what to do by morning. Angry and exhausted but not distraught, Carol got in the shower to start her day. She figured dominating a few submissives may clear her mind enough to develop an ideal strategy.

XIII

Chapter 13

When Carol arrived at work, she was in an overly frustrated mood and was all too willing to dole her aggressions out on her clients.

Eric, a strong and stout masochistic man, was the first appointment of the day which delighted Carol. His affinity for pain knew no limits, and this was the type of person who was essential in Carol's healing.

At two minutes past his ten o'clock appointment, Eric pressed the buzzer to alert Carol of his arrival.

"I cannot believe you dare to keep me waiting! That kind of audacity is intolerable!"

"I'm sorry, Mistress Carol. I had a flat tire on my way here." Eric explained.

"What do I hate even more than having my time wasted?"

"Excuses." Eric sheepishly replied.

"You will be punished for your actions!"

"Yes, Mistress Carol," Eric enthusiastically replied with a smile on his face.

"From now on, you will address me as Lady Carol. I am nobody's mistress! Understand?"

"Yes, Lady Carol."

The change in her title was due to her hatred of John having a mistress. She felt that she works in a palace, sits on a throne, and has earned the dignity that comes with the title Lady.

"Don't forget to put on your chastity device before entering my kingdom." Carol reminded Eric as she granted him access to the changing area.

Although clients could disrobe to whatever level they felt comfortable with, Carol had a strict requirement for a chastity device to be worn by any man that may become aroused during a session. Seeing a man's erection didn't bother her but knowing that a submissive enjoyed the abuse interfered with the pleasure she received from the session. In Carol's mind, their suffering was for her amusement and not for their perverted desires.

As Carol waited for Eric, she sat on her throne and watched him quickly undress on a nearby monitor. It was evident that he was eager to feel the sting of her crop almost as much as Carol had a desire to flog him. So, when Eric was ready and positioned in front of the chamber door, Carol immediately pressed the button on her throne to let him enter.

When Eric entered Carol's new dungeon, he was in awe. The bright and ornate space was utterly foreign compared to the dark and solemn dungeons he was accustomed to.

As he paused to absorb his unfamiliar surroundings, Carol redirected his attention by saying, "You may approach."

Eric slowly walked towards the throne that Carol was

perched atop while making a mental note of the various equipment strewn about the room, some of which he was surprised to see that Carol had.

"Stop!" Carol shouted as he got within ten feet of her. "You will never approach any closer than you currently are unless directed to do so. You will also bow to me then kneel to await further instructions from me. Failure to follow these rules may be cause for immediate removal from my palace. Do you understand?"

Eric bowed, kneeled before her, and said, "Yes, Mistress Carol."

An enraged Carol unhooked a coiled whip from the side of her throne and cracked it less than a foot over his head, screaming, "Do I look like a mistress? Do you think I am a homewrecking whore?"

"No, Lady Carol. Please forgive me for my ignorance."

"I should throw you out of my palace for the disrespect that you have shown me."

"I request that you accept my sincere apology, Lady Carol. I cannot express how sorry I am for my inconsiderateness."

"Are you asking me for something? Are you allowed to want or ask for anything from me?" Carol questioned Eric.

"I am unworthy to desire anything, Lady Carol. I am merely begging to be allowed to continue serving you. Your happiness is the only thing that matters. I made an error in my servitude, and I assure you I will not make the same mistake again."

"What are you willing to do to show me that your apology is genuine?"

"Anything you desire, Lady Carol."

Carol stood up, grabbed a riding crop off the arm of her throne, and approached Eric, saying, "If this is the truth that you're speaking, follow me."

Eric stood up and took one step before he felt the sting of Carol's crop landing against his abdomen, causing him to slump forward in pain.

"You are a disrespectful animal and shall crawl on all fours like one!"

Eric dutifully complied and continued following Carol across the room to a metal cage that was four feet wide, four feet long, and three feet high with a three-foot rubber pad partly lining the bottom of the enclosure.

"Get in the cage, you filthy pig!" Carol instructed.

For a moment, Eric hesitated due to his claustrophobia, causing Carol to land another crop strike, this time across his exposed buttocks.

"Are you going to make me repeat myself?" Carol asked.

"I do not wish to disobey your orders, but I have claustrophobia, Lady Carol," Eric explained.

"You were the one who said that you would do anything that makes me happy. Ultimately, it's your decision, but keep in mind that you can and will be removed from my stable very quickly.

Eric tried to calm himself and enter the cage but only got halfway into it before stopping as another brutal smack landed again on his buttocks.

He instinctively wanted to shout out his safeword, but Eric knew that meant he would indeed be eliminated as a client. So, he begrudgingly continued into the cage.

"Stay on the rubber mat. I'd hate for something bad to happen to you." Carol said with an evil laugh.

With Eric hunched over on all fours and his eyes tightly shut in an attempt to ignore his cramped quarters, Carol closed the gate.

"Now, it's in your best interest to remail still," Carol said as she hooked up wires from a twelve-volt high ampere lithium battery to the cage. "Or not. It is your decision if you wish to amuse me by touching the cage." She said as she made her way back to her throne.

With Carol lost in her thoughts, fifteen minutes had unknowingly passed before Eric's moans caught her attention.

As Carol went to the cage, she asked, "Are you uncomfortable?"

To which Eric replied," Yes, Lady Carol."

"Good! Do you want me to let you out?"

"My only desire is to serve you," Eric grunted out.

"Then why are you moaning so emphatically? Does it not please you to please me?"

"I do enjoy pleasing you, but I have a cramp in my leg," Eric replied with his eyes still firmly shut.

"Look at me when you speak to me!" Carol shouted as she hit the side of the cage with her hand forgetting that it had an electrical current running through it. "You bastard! You just shocked me!"

"I apologize, Lady Carol. It is my ignorance that caused you pain, and I accept full responsibility for it."

"You're damn right that it's your fault. You don't need to remind me of the fact." Carol hissed back in response.

Carol yanked the wires from the cage and opened the gate, telling Eric, "Exit the cage!"

Eric scampered out as quickly as possible and laid prostrate on the floor, attempting to stretch his leg cramp out.

"Does it still hurt?"

"Yes, Lady Carol," Eric replied while trying to rub his hamstring.

"I can help with that," Carol said as she cuffed his hands behind his back.

A three-foot spreader bar was placed between Eric's legs and secured to his ankles before Carol lowered a cable from an overhead pulley.

"You will be good as new in just a few minutes," Carol told him as she attached the cable to the spreader bar.

With the press of a button, Eric was dragged across the floor before being hoisted into the air upside-down.

"That should stretch you out a bit." Carol laughed. "While I'm waiting for you to feel better, I may as well practice my whipping skills."

Carol gave him a little shove, and Eric began swinging left to right.

"I feel better already, Lady Carol," Eric said with hopes of being lowered back down to the floor.

"Just a little longer. You don't want to rush a good stretch. You may get injured." Carol said while retrieving the whip from her throne.

With a flick of her wrist, the whip was sent towards its target and cracked just to the left of Eric's torso, causing him to writhe around to avoid the painful bite.

"Stop moving around!" Carol ordered him as she swung the whip again, missing Eric to the right this time.

With Eric's face now turning purple from the blood rushing to his head, he pleaded for Carol to let him down. "Lady Carol, I feel like I'm going to throw up."

"If you vomit on my floor, you will pay a severe price!" Carol told him as she gave Eric another push to swing him with more velocity. "I thought you said that you would do anything I asked of you?"

"I did say that, Lady Carol."

"So you lied to me!" Carol shouted as she hit his ribs with her crop.

"I thought I could endure everything, but I am not as strong as I thought I was."

"Then say the magic word. That is all it takes for your suffering to stop."

"Please," Eric said with slurred speech, nearly at the point of passing out.

"That's not the word," Carol said while landing another strike on his back.

Eric mumbled his safeword, "Pumpkin."

Carol immediately lowered him to the ground and ended the session. After releasing him from his bondage, Eric laid motionless on the floor, and Carol went back to her throne.

After a few minutes, Eric made it to his feet and approached Carol. Ten feet away from her, Eric bowed and kneeled before her.

"What are you doing?" Carol asked.

"I am begging for forgiveness for not doing what I told you that I could do. You are a strong and powerful woman that I hold in the highest esteem. I know with your continued training, I can learn to suffer through your most significant punishments." Eric told Carol.

"Why should I show compassion for you? You continually disappoint me but expect me to forgive you? I have someone in my life that I have forgiven multiple times, yet he has not learned his lesson. He will never change who he is, and you will never change who you are. You are pathetic."

"Yes, Lady Carol." Eric humbly said before leaving the dungeon.

Again, Carol watched Eric on the monitor as he was getting changed. She could see the sadness on his face. The exuberant demeanor he had when he arrived had dissipated entirely. Carol couldn't help but feel some remorse for kicking him out. However, she kept reminding herself that he was the one that didn't live up to his end of the agreement. In her palace, she had to rule with an iron fist. Showing weakness was not an option. That was one of the first rules Lisa had taught her. If you showed weakness, it would ruin the submissive's experience, yet it was apparent that she had ruined the experience for both herself and Eric by not showing compassion.

Eric pressed the buzzer so he could leave Carol's dungeon. For a moment, Carol thought about calling him back into her palace to have a discussion with him regarding her expectations and what his limitations are, but she didn't know if that would be proper. She doesn't want to show weakness, but she also knew that she needed a submissive like him for her healing.

Rather than just letting Eric leave her stable of submissives, Carol told him over the intercom, "If you regret your actions, you are free to reapply for a position in my palace."

"Yes, Lady Carol. I sincerely apologize for disappointing you and will reapply as soon as I get home."

"Do not view this as a weakness of mine. I am not guaranteeing you a position, just an opportunity to reapply."

"It is an honor to have you consider my application as it has been an honor to serve you, Lady Carol."

Carol pressed the door release button for Eric to exit the premises. When the door closed behind Eric, Carol sensed a desolateness growing within her that she had not experienced in many months. She couldn't understand why she felt that way since the only change that had occurred was losing a client, of which she had plenty. Nonetheless, Carol felt depressed and lonely. Because of this, she resorted back to her old ways of coping with these dark emotions.

With a few taps on her phone, Carol ordered a feast fit for a queen and arranged for a food delivery service to bring it to her. As she waited, Carol began cleaning her new and still pristine palace, but it felt more like a burdensome process than a remedial one as it once had in the past.

Forty-five minutes later, the buzzer for the backdoor went off. Carol could tell from a glance at the monitor that it was the food delivery service.

Not wanting anyone outside of her clientele to know what her place of business is, Carol said through the intercom, "Please leave the food at the back door. Someone will retrieve it in a few minutes."

When the delivery person left, Carol brought in the three bags of food and arranged everything in a buffet-style on a table in her palace. She had a selection of grilled artichoke, fried calamari, crispy Brussel sprouts with goat cheese, chicken piccata, seafood linguini, a cheddar brisket burger, and for dessert crème brulee and tiramisu.

Rather than putting a selection of food on a paper plate to enjoy in her favorite chair, Carol grabbed a fork and started gulping down mouthfuls of food to satisfy the emptiness within. With every indulgent bite, Carol had hoped to appease the gloomy disposition that had manifested itself. However, after devouring most of the meals and half of the dessert, Carol didn't feel any better than she did before. If anything, she felt worse, having a now engorged stomach pressing against a tight corset that she couldn't remove due to having clients arriving soon.

Carol cleaned up the remnants of food and sat on her throne, waiting for her next appointment to arrive. She fought off the inclination to nap with every elapsing minute as her body tried to process the vast amount of food she consumed. Being only halfway alert to her surroundings, Carol was startled when Andrew pressed the entrance buzzer.

"What do you want?" Carol shouted through the intercom.

"Only to serve you, Mistress Carol," Andrew replied.

"Why do all of you worthless slaves refer to me as a mistress?"

"I will call you whatever you desire. Would Goddess be preferable to you?"

"Lady Carol will suffice."

"Yes, Lady Carol. I think that is a very proper title for you." Andrew acknowledged.

"It doesn't matter what you think, simply do not refer to

me as anything other than a lady," Carol instructed him before granting access to her palace.

As always, Andrew deposited his payment, undressed to his boxer briefs, and waited patiently for Carol to allow entrance to the dungeon area. However, his wait seemed much longer than usual. About ten minutes had passed when he began wondering if the buzzer was working, but pressing it again would surely infuriate Carol, so he continued to display patience.

Unknowingly to Andrew, Carol was in the bathroom purging the large feast that she had for lunch. Her body was not accustomed to such a vast amount of food any longer. Eventually, Carol returned to her throne and granted Andrew access.

"Your new place is lovely, Lady Carol. Your beauty is the only thing that rivals it." Andrew said as he walked in.

"You have always been my favorite, Andrew. That is why after I run down the new rules, I am granting you a special privilege for the day."

Just as she did with Eric, Carol stopped Andrew at the range of ten feet from her throne and made him bow and kneel. With Andrew on his knees, Carol reminded him to only refer to her as Lady Carol before further instructing him of her guidelines and expectations.

"Are you fully aware of what is required of you to remain a part of my stable?" Carol asked.

"Yes, Lady Carol," Andrew replied.

"Then you may approach my throne."

Standing before Carol, Andrew asked, "What can I do to please you, Lady Carol?"

"I'm not feeling well today, so I'm going to grant you the privilege of massaging my feet."

Andrew knelt and asked, "May I please take your foot into my hands, Lady Carol?"

"You may," Carol said as she lifted her right foot off the ground. "Do not get aroused because I have allowed your filthy paws to touch me."

"I won't, Lady Carol. I would never disrespect you in such a manner."

"Today will be a fabulous day for you if you continue to serve me properly. We have another submissive attending the session today.

"That is wonderful, Lady Carol."

"Yes, it is. The best part is that you will assist me since I am feeling slightly ill."

"I would be honored by aiding you in any fashion you desire, Lady Carol."

"See, this is why I give you the extraordinary benefit of massaging my feet. No other slave is ever allowed to touch me without being immediately removed from my palace."

"I understand and am humbled by your graciousness, Lady Carol."

Carol switched her feet and told Andrew, "I asked you to massage my feet, not molest them. Add a little more pressure."

Andrew obliged and continued massaging Carol's feet without saying a word for the next twenty minutes before Carol said, "My new pet will be arriving shortly. It's time you take your place in the kennel."

Andrew immediately released Carol's foot, backed away

from her with his head lowered until beyond the ten-foot radius, then made his way directly to the cage. After locking him in, Carol returned to her throne and awaited her new sub's arrival.

XIV

Chapter 14

At ten minutes before two, the buzzer rang again with someone at the back door. This time it was a mid-twenties woman with long flowing blonde hair, which Carol assumed was her new submissive.

"State your purpose for pressing the buzzer," Carol said.

"My name is Deedra. I am here for a two o'clock appointment."

"Why are you so early?"

"So I can be ready by two o'clock and avoid keeping you waiting for me," Deedra replied.

"Huh, how thoughtful. However, I expect you to be punctual and arrive at your appointment time. You can prepare yourself for the session on the time you are paying for rather than getting an extra ten minutes in my palace."

"I understand. Please forgive me." Deedra said.

"I will look past it this time and will send a stablemate out to run through my requirements and expectations since I'm tired of repeating myself. You may enter." Carol said as she pressed the latch release.

As Carol opened the cage door to let Andrew out, she asked, "You do remember all of my rules, don't you?"

"Yes, Lady Carol."

"Good. I expect you will thoroughly explain everything to the new submissive. Any insubordination on her part will cause you to suffer the punishment for her. Understood?"

"Yes, Lady Carol."

Andrew entered the changing room as Carol watched and listened to their interaction on the monitor. Carol noticed Deedra had an uncanny similarity to Kayla. The blonde hair, the petite body, it all seemed so familiar to her. For a moment, Carol thought that it might be fun after all to chastise this woman.

"Hi, I'm Andrew." He said with an outstretched hand.

"I'm Deedra."

"It's a pleasure to meet you. Lady Carol asked me to run through all of the requirements. You must adhere to all of the rules, or I will endure your punishment, and her punishments can be rather extreme, so I ask that you follow all of the directions."

"Watching you get punished sounds like fun," Deedra said with a deviant giggle.

Andrew leaned against the lockers with his arm folded and said, "You're going to be a handful, aren't you?"

"I suppose I can be. I am more of a brat with mommy issues than a submissive. I have the mindset that rules are meant to be broken, not followed."

"Does Lady Carol know this?"

"I assume she does. I said on the application that I was a bratty submissive." Deedra told Andrew as she began to undress.

"Please follow her directions. I can only handle so much, and as I said, her discipline has become more stringent." Andrew pleaded.

"I'll see what I can do, but I'm not making any promises," Deedra said with a wink and a smile. "How long have you been coming here?"

"About five or six months. Lady Carol is a wonderful dominatrix, and I feel close to her, so it's a good fit."

A smile formed on Carol's face when she heard Andrew speak so highly of her on the monitor. Especially when he said he felt close to her. She understood that they have a professional relationship, but she felt close to Andrew as well. Knowing that the feelings were mutual just made the bond they shared that much stronger.

"What are you doing after your session?" Deedra asked.

"I don't have any plans. Why?"

"I thought maybe we could get together and have a drink afterward."

"I don't know. I do have some business matters to attend to."

"Okay. It's your decision, but you should know that I can be quite the brat." Deedra said as she took off her bra.

"Are you trying to blackmail me?"

"Never! I am merely encouraging you to make the correct decision."

"Fine, I'll have one drink with you, but you better be on your best behavior during the session," Andrew said.

Carol, hearing Andrew admit his feelings towards her then deciding on having drinks with another woman, infuriated her.

"Andrew, get in here this instant," Carol shouted over the intercom.

Andrew immediately rushed back to Carol, leaving Deedra to finish getting ready.

"What were you doing in the changing room?"

"I was going over the rules of your palace, Lady Carol."

"Was that all? Because it looked to me like the two of you were engaged in flirtatious behavior."

"I admit she is an appealing woman, but I do not desire her. My only desire is to serve you."

"In time, we shall see who you will choose to serve. For now, back in your cage!"

As soon as Carol locked the gate, Deedra rang the buzzer to come in.

"I can't wait to see in person the slut you seem so infatuated with," Carol told Andrew while returning to her throne and pressing the latch release.

Deedra came in wearing only a pair of thong panties. Her confidence was on complete display as she boldly strolled through Carol's palace, seemingly unimpressed with Carol's décor. But as she approached Carol's throne, she did bow and kneel before her.

"Is this the first impression you wish to make? Coming into my palace looking like a stripper says a lot about what kind of a tramp you are!"

"Well, your website said that I could disrobe to whatever

level I feel comfortable with for the session, Lady Carol," Deedra replied.

"Yes, that is factual. I just figured you would display some modesty."

"I did. I kept my panties on." Deedra said in a cynical tone.

"You are quite a contemptuous little girl."

"You have a pretty nice place here, Carol. I mean, it's not like other dungeons, but it will suffice."

"Your disrespect will not be tolerated! Did Andrew not tell you how to address me and what my rules are?"

"Yeah, he did."

"Then why are you not appropriately referring to me as Lady Carol?"

Deedra shrugged her shoulders and said, "I don't know."

"That is it! I'm done with your attitude. You will learn some manners, or you'll be ejected from my palace."

Carol unlocked the cage door, and as Andrew crawled out, Carol said, "I told you that you were responsible for her not following orders. Did you or did you not tell her how to address me appropriately?"

"I did, Lady Carol. She told me she was a brat and..."

"Are you making excuses for her?"

"No, Lady Carol."

"Turn around and prepare for your punishment," Carol told Andrew as she grabbed the crop from her throne.

Andrew complied and interlocked his fingers behind his head, waiting for her fury to be unleashed on him. Carol swung the crop as hard as she could, and the palace echoed with the snap it made when it hit the flesh of Andrew's buttocks. Andrew's fingers came off the back of his head, but he never dropped his hands below his shoulders.

"That was for her not addressing me correctly. This next one is for her disrespect."

Carol swung again, but the rod of the crop made more contact than the tip causing Andrew to yelp in response to the added discomfort. The release of Carol's anger calmed her until she heard Deedra giggling.

"What are you laughing at?" Carol asked Deedra. "Do you think it's funny that Andrew is being punished for your misconduct?"

"It's quite amusing."

"Well, don't you think for a second that you are going to escape any punishment yourself. I rule this palace with an iron fist, but I do believe to be fair with my discipline."

"Yes, Lady Carol." A now mild-mannered Deedra responded.

"Get up and go to that kneeling bench," Carol ordered Deedra. "Andrew, get me the wooden paddle off the wall by the cage."

Deedra stood before the kneeling bench, knowing full well what was about to happen and as she waited to feel the punishment Carol had in store for her, the excitement caused her to shake her ass in anticipation.

"Kneel on the bench and press your thighs firmly against the pad in front of them," Carol instructed Deedra before securing the straps around her calves and thighs to prevent any attempt to avoid the punishment. "Now lean over the bench."

Deedra complied by bending over at the waist and laying her torso flat against the wooden plank as Carol secured another strap around the middle of Deedra's back to prevent her from rising off the bench when the paddle strikes her buttocks.

"One last thing, dear. I have to cuff your hands to the legs of the bench to make sure you don't get your pretty little fingers hurt by putting them in the path of my paddle." Carol said as she began securing Deedra's wrists. "This is a must because I am going to teach you some manners one way or another. By the end of this, you will obey me!"

Carol took a step back from Deedra, who was now fully restrained, as Andrew eagerly handed her the paddle for Deedra's punishment to commence. However, Carol was nearly repulsed with just a single look at a woman's ass in the air. No matter how mad she was at Deedra, she couldn't bring herself to smack her with the paddle.

"Here," Carol said to Andrew while handing him the paddle. "I think you should administer the punishment. She thought it was funny when you were punished. Now I want to be amused watching her be punished."

"But I don't..."

"You don't have a choice," Carol said as she went back to her throne. "Ten swats with the paddle and make them count, Andrew. If you do not punish her appropriately, I will punish both of you beyond your tolerance levels until you call out your safeword! And you know what will happen if you use your safeword, don't you?"

"Yes, Lady Carol," Andrew replied.

"What are you waiting for, Andrew? Swat her ass!" Carol commanded.

Andrew summoned all of his aggression as he raised the

paddle. Carol enthusiastically waited for the unmistakable sound of flesh being compressed rapidly under the paddle, followed by a whimper of pain, but it never happened.

"Do I need to remind you of the pain she caused you? I will gladly administer more of it to you if your memory needs to be refreshed."

"No, Lady Carol. I am fully aware of why I was punished."

"Then what are you waiting for? I command you to swat her ass."

Andrew stood silently, staring at Deedra's sculpted buttocks and milky white flesh, but he couldn't bring himself to send the paddle agonizingly flying into her.

"You worthless, puny man. Do as I say and hit her. Damn it, hit her, John!" Carol shouted out as Andrew looked at her in confusion.

Carol rose in anger off her throne, grabbed a cat o' nine tails whip off the wall, and made her way to Andrew.

"Turn around. You are going to pay for your insubordination."

Carol swung the whip, and every tail landed across Andrew's back, sending him to his knees in pain. Then Carol turned her attention to Deedra and landed several blows across her back and ass as she let out a shriek.

"Get on your feet, slave!" Carol commanded Andrew.

Before his legs straightened out, Carol landed another strike of the whip across his back, sending him back to his hands and knees.

In agony, Andrew yelled out his safeword, "Marshmallow!"

"I am so sick and tired of your antics. Acting as if I was the most meaningful person in your life while you make a date with another woman! You repulse me, John!" Carol screamed right before kicking Andrew between his legs, the toe of her boot landing squarely against his scrotum.

Andrew cried out in pain, "Please stop. I can't do this." while holding his crotch.

"I can't do this either! Get out of here and take your home-wrecking whore with you!" Carol shouted as she sat down on her throne.

Andrew crawled over to Deedra, unfastened her from her restraints, and they made their way to the exit.

"I don't ever want to see either of you in my palace again. Don't waste my time by applying for readmission either." Carol told them as she pressed the latch release. "Get your belongings and immediately vacate the premises."

Andrew and Deedra grabbed their clothes from the lockers and immediately left. They didn't know what to expect if they delayed their departure too long, so they got dressed outside in the parking lot.

"That was insane! Are you okay?" Deedra asked.

"Yeah, I'll be okay. I don't know what has gotten into her. She used to be the best dominatrix in town, but I think she's out of control."

"Why did she call you John in there?"

"I have no idea, but whoever he is, he has pissed her off. I could use that drink if you're still up for it."

"Absolutely! I think we both could use a drink after that psychotic outburst."

As Andrew and Deedra left, Carol remained seated on her throne, crying uncontrollably. Carol knew she was losing control of her actions, but what feared her the most was that she was once again beginning to think she was losing her mind. Everything that transpired during that session played back in Carol's head repeatedly, mainly the part with her calling Andrew by her husband's name and equating Deedra to Kayla.

Carol knew this couldn't continue. She had to find a way to stop the insanity that was creeping upon her, but how? There was little time left for her to convince John to leave Kayla and stay married to her. It was impossible to lose enough weight for John to find her desirable within the next couple of days. It was probably too late for that option anyway since he had already proposed. Carol also couldn't turn back the hands of time and be twenty years younger to compete on that level either. It was evident that she had lost every battle with John, but there was one front the war had not raged upon, his precious little Kayla.

Carol canceled the rest of her appointments to focus on removing Kayla from her life once and for all. Over the next few hours, Carol sat amongst her palace's silence, trying to decide what her most forceful elements of battle were and her best angle of attack because having a heart-to-heart talk with Kayla wouldn't change a thing. Carol knew that she had one last offensive to launch, and it would have to be an all-out war.

The plan slowly came to life in Carol's mind. Every detail had to be strategically planned and every variable considered for this to be a success. It would take time for a plan like that to come together, but that was the one thing Carol didn't have, so some minor details would have to be forgone to put her strategy into action as quickly as possible. It had to start with Lisa, and although Carol despised lying to her, she had no choice.

"Hey, girl," Lisa said, answering Carol's call.

"Can I come over so we can talk?"

"I'm getting ready to go out on date number two with William, but I can spare a few minutes. What's going on?"

"It's John," Carol said with a shaky voice. "My marriage is over!" she continued, trying her best to sound distressed.

"I'm canceling my plans. Where are you? I'll come right over."

"I don't want you to cancel your plans. I'll be okay." Carol said with a sniffle.

"That's nonsense! You know I will always be there for you. Besides, I just sent William a text and told him I had to cancel."

"Are you sure you don't mind?"

"Not at all. Where do you want me to pick you up at?"

"I'll head over to your house," Carol told Lisa.

"Hon, I don't think you are in any condition to drive."

"I'll be okay. I have to get away from here anyway."

"I'll be waiting for you. Drive safely, and if you don't think you can make it to my place, call me. I'll come to get you."

"Thanks, Lisa. See you soon."

Carol left the smeared mascara on her face to emphasize that she had been crying and headed to Lisa's house. On the drive over, she practiced her lines like an actress preparing for the opening night of a Broadway play. Lisa knew her better than anyone, and Carol knew she had to convince Lisa or the entirety of her plan was going to fail.

When Carol arrived, Lisa said, "Hon, I didn't know what

you wanted to drink, so I have water boiling for tea, a bottle of wine, or if you need something stronger, a bottle of vodka chilling in the freezer."

"You didn't have to go to all this trouble. I just needed a shoulder to lean on." Carol softly said.

"It isn't any trouble. I always have wine ready and vodka in the freezer. So, what's your poison?"

"Vodka and cranberry juice if you have it."

"You must be upset. I don't think I've seen you opt for hard liquor in years."

"Things are bad, and I am at a total loss as to what I should do."

"Start from the beginning, and let's see if we can figure something out," Lisa said while handing Carol her drink.

"Well, it all started last night when Mark came over to my house." Carol began.

"Mark? Belle's ex-boyfriend?"

Carol nodded her head.

"What was he doing at your house?" Lisa asked.

"He came to tell me about the affair John was having. I guess he's friends with Kayla."

"Well, that isn't news to you. You knew about her. What made you so upset?"

"He told me that he felt I should know that John asked Kayla to marry him."

"No!"

"...and she said yes," Carol said as she broke down in tears.

"Honey, I am so sorry. Do you want to move in here with me for a while?"

"Mark said that John and Kayla are leaving Monday for a

vacation to celebrate their engagement, so I have some time to think about if I'll need a place to stay. Right now, I just need to clear my head."

"Why don't you stay here with me. Do you think it's a good idea to be in that house all alone?"

"No, I don't want to be in that house at all right now. That's why I think I need a vacation as well. Go someplace where I can relax and think things through."

"That sounds like a great idea. I can clear my schedule for a few days and go with you!" Lisa said.

"I hope you're not offended, but I feel like this is something I need to do alone. Just be by myself and lost in my thoughts."

"I get that it seems like a good idea, but I'm worried about you. I don't think you should be alone." Lisa told Carol.

"I'll be okay. If I start to have a nervous breakdown, I promise I will call you. It appears that I'll have to learn how to make decisions on my own from now on, so I feel like I should start immediately. Does that make sense?"

"Okay, but you promise to call me if you need anything?"

"You will be the first person that I will call. I promise!"

"Where are you going to go?" Lisa asked.

"I was thinking about jumping in my car and drive where the wind will take me. I don't need to stay anywhere fancy. I only need to be alone with my thoughts."

"When are you leaving?"

"First thing tomorrow," Carol replied.

"Are you staying with me tonight?"

"No, I need to cancel my appointments for the next couple of weeks and pack some things for my trip."

"Then grab your computer and some clothes from home, come back here, cancel your appointments, and stay the night with me. You don't need to stay in that house a minute longer than you have to." Lisa told her.

Realizing that Lisa wasn't going to give up on the thought of having her spend the night, Carol finally agreed to stay.

XV

Chapter 15

Saturday morning, Carol started the day by making a pot of coffee to take with her on the road. Smelling the coffee brewing, Lisa came downstairs to spend a little time with her best friend before she left.

"You're up bright and early," Lisa said.

"I wanted to get an early start on the road."

"Do you have any idea where you are heading to?"

"Not a clue, but anywhere has to be better than here," Carol replied.

"I still don't like to think about you roaming around without any idea of where you're going. Especially feeling the way that you do."

"I'll be fine. Stop worrying."

"Do you know when you will be back at least?" Lisa asked.

"In a week. Maybe two at the most. I want to have everything figured out before John comes back from his vacation. I'll get hold of you as soon as I come back."

"Or if you need anything, right?"

"Right," Carol said as she filled up her large travel mug with coffee.

"I'm going to miss you while you're gone."

"Me too. Just remember that I'm very thankful for having a friend like you to count on. You have meant the world to me."

"I feel like I'm not doing enough to help you," Lisa said.

"You've done more than enough already. After every affair John had, you were there for me. It's time that I handle things on my own. Everyone has to grow up at some point."

"I love you. Be safe." Lisa shouted as Carol got in the car.

Carol pulled out of the driveway, but she wasn't heading out of town. It never was her intention to leave. She only had to make a quick stop at the hardware store to pick up a couple of things before heading back to her palace to put her plan into action.

The first item on her checklist was to set up the industrial floor fan Carol purchased. Then she secured a lawn sprinkler above the pulley system and ran a hose from the bathroom's faucet to the sprinkler. Lastly, Carol attached a one-hundred-foot rope to one of the overhead pulleys.

Well into the late afternoon, Carol carefully selected which tools she would need to achieve her desired result. There wasn't a need for the soft leather whips or the more playful toys because this wasn't going to be for fun, at least not for Kayla, so she made sure to have all of her chosen equipment close at hand and discarded the rest out of the way in the corner of the dungeon. She also needed to ensure a direct pathway from the entrance to the center of her palace, so she pushed the benches, tables, and miscellaneous equipment out of the way. By early evening, Carol had everything in perfect order to commence her well-planned and foolproof offensive. The only thing left to do was to wait for the ideal time to launch the attack.

Having realized that she hasn't had anything to eat all day, Carol decided to get some dinner. She didn't want to risk being seen in town since she was supposed to be on vacation, and having a food delivery service wouldn't be an ideal choice either since she wanted to have an alibi established for her whereabouts. With just a couple of granola bars to tide her over on the three-hour drive, Carol headed to Santa Maria to visit her aunt.

Carol thought her Aunt Cora was an excellent choice due to her age-related feeble-mindedness. Aunt Cora was still able to live alone and could remember most things that were not time-related. That being the case, Carol knew that Aunt Cora, if asked, would tell authorities that Carol did visit and would probably repeat any time Carol told her aunt that she had arrived as well as left.

It was about half-past eight when Carol arrived at her aunt's house. While Carol sat in her car, flashbacks of the simpler times of childhood flashed through her mind. She would spend one month every summer at her aunt's house. Carol could remember all the neighborhood children's names and the games they played, recalled having water balloon fights in the yard with her aunt, and sitting on her uncle's lap while he read her bedtime stories every night. A tear began to form in the corner of Carol's eye because she missed him so much. Although he passed away about ten years ago, it was still fresh in her mind, and it felt like it was just last month that Carol lost the greatest man she had ever known. She had always wanted to marry a man just like him. Of course, she didn't.

After gathering her composure, Carol knocked on her aunt's door.

"Caroline, my baby girl! How are you?" Aunt Cora said while hugging Carol.

"I'm doing well. I thought I would pop over for a surprise visit. I hope you don't mind."

"I don't mind one bit. It is always such a pleasure to see you. Come in."

"Your house looks exactly as I remember it," Carol said.

"That's because I am too damn old to be moving furniture and pictures around."

"Aunt Cora, you will never be old. You probably still go outside and play with all of the children like you used to."

"I do. It is such a joy to play with the children of the kids you grew up alongside. They all call me grandma, but I can't keep up with them anymore."

"Time can be a bitch," Carol told her aunt.

"Caroline, you watch your language!"

"Sorry, Aunt Cora."

"Are you hungry? I have some leftover pot roast."

"I would love some. Thank you."

Aunt Cora made a plate of food for Carol, and they sat at the kitchen table talking about the good times of the past as Carol ate. However, every time Aunt Cora would ask about Carol's job, her husband, or anything else currently going on in her life, Carol would change the topic back to the memories she had of when she was a child. Carol wanted to escape from the painful reality that preyed upon her vulnerable mind, if only for one night.

When Carol finished her dinner, Aunt Cora asked, "Caroline, would you like to spend the night here, or do you have to leave?"

"I would love to spend the night with you if that's okay."

"It has been such a long time since I didn't have to sleep in an empty house. I'll put some fresh linens on the bed for you."

"You don't have to do that, Aunt Cora. I'll take care of it." Carol told her.

"You said it yourself. I'm not old yet. I can handle it."

After Cora cleaned up the dishes, she walked into the living room and paused for a moment.

"Aunt Cora, is everything okay?"

"Yes, dear. I just seemed to have forgotten what I was looking for."

"Maybe you're just a little tired. We have been visiting for quite some time." Carol said.

"That's probably it. I'm going to lay down and get some rest. Help yourself to something to eat if you're hungry."

"Thank you, Aunt Cora. Sweet dreams. I'll see you in the morning."

Carol grabbed a book off a shelf before retreating to the guest room, where she tried to recreate her fondest memory of her uncle reading her a bedtime story. Carol even gave each character a silly voice, just like he did. Hours would pass before sleepiness sat in and for Carol to be able to drift off to dreamland.

Six o'clock Sunday morning, Carol started her day like any

other by making a pot of coffee. The smell wafted through the house, waking Aunt Cora up from a restful sleep.

As Aunt Cora entered the kitchen, she was startled by Carol's presence and said, "My goodness, Caroline. You scared the dickens out of me. When did you get here?"

"Yesterday, Aunt Cora. We had dinner together. Remember?"

"Oh, yes. I remember. We had pot roast for dinner. That was delicious, wasn't it?"

"It was the best that I have had in years. Even better than mine."

"Caroline, you are too sweet. I'm sorry for being a little foggy-headed. I'm like that until I have my morning coffee."

"Well, let's get a cup in you," Carol said as she poured a mug for her aunt.

After they finished their coffee, Carol said, "I better get going, Aunt Cora. But thank you for letting me spend the night with you."

"Where are you off to in such a rush, Caroline?"

"I'm not heading anywhere in particular. I'll probably head up the coast a little further and take in some sightseeing. Maybe do a little camping."

"I appreciate you spending some time with me. I miss you so much!"

"I've missed you too, Aunt Cora," Carol said as she hugged her aunt.

"Come back and visit me soon. If you let me know when you're coming, I'll prepare something special for dinner."

"I'll do that. I love you, Aunt Cora." Carol said as she made her way to the car.

"I love you too, my sweet baby girl!"

Leaving was a bittersweet moment for Carol. She found comfort and contentment staying with her aunt and wanted it to last forever. Still, Carol knew she had to take care of the situation she left behind because it was impossible to relive her childhood forever.

Carol returned to her palace around noon and sat upon her throne. The perfection of a royal residence that once radiated around her appeared tarnished, somewhat like the crumbling walls of an unkept castle. You can tell that it possessed a regal refinement at one time, but it now looks like it is a mere fraction of its previous elegance to Carol. However, she shrugged it off as only being due to moving the unused equipment to the side of the room. She figured it would regain its palatial glory once again after she wins the war.

Refocusing on the task at hand, Carol knew John would attend his usual Sunday Night Football party the guys typically had when the Oakland Raiders played and that it was only for the guys where they smoked cigars, drank, and shouted at the television. There were no women allowed at these events, so as long as Kayla didn't have any plans, she would surely be home alone.

After setting the air conditioner in her palace to sixty degrees, Carol drove to Pasadena to keep an eye on Kayla until the moment presented itself to grab her. She knew that doing it in broad daylight was risky, but she also trusted that her instincts would kick in when it was the right time. However, as she drove by Kayla's house, Carol noticed that her car wasn't in the driveway, so she continued down the street to avoid neighbor's detecting a strange vehicle parked outside of the residence.

The thought occurred to Carol that maybe Kayla was at work, so she headed to Sporty's. With one swoop through the parking lot, Carol spotted the car and pulled into an open spot directly in front of the large windows that lined the building's front wall. There she watched Kayla for about an hour flirt with the other men in the bar. Her slutty behavior possibly was because she was hoping for a big tip which made Carol think that Kayla was only playing John for his money and attention. If that is the case, why then would she have agreed to marry John? Either way, for love or money, Carol knew Kayla had to be removed from her and John's lives.

Eventually, Carol moved her car to a back corner of the lot and waited for Kayla to get off work. It took a couple of hours, but Kayla finally exited the bar, and as she pulled out of the parking lot, Carol was right behind her, excitedly trailing every movement she made.

As they got to Pasadena, Kayla made a stop at the grocery store, which angered Carol. She just wanted to get this done and move on with her life, but Kayla wasn't cooperating. Fifteen minutes later, Kayla came out of the grocery store and continued down the road to her home.

Carol drove around the block one time so Kayla wouldn't notice her pulling up to the house. Carol's nerves were a mess, and a massive amount of adrenaline was coursing through her veins, but the time still didn't feel right to approach the house. Ten minutes later, her instincts were proven correct as another car pulled into Kayla's driveway.

It was another young woman, most likely a friend of

Kayla's, carrying a bottle of liquor. Carol had a feeling that it was going to be a long wait for the friend to leave, even if she left at all before John was likely to show up. If that were the case, everything Carol had planned was for nothing. The war would be over with, and Kayla would be victorious.

The thought of abducting both of them crossed her mind, but Carol didn't have an issue with Kayla's friend and didn't want to hurt anybody that didn't need to make amends. However, Carol grew more impatient over time and was on the verge of making a terrible decision to enter the house, taking on both of the women inside. So, she decided to drive to a fast-food restaurant to get some dinner and try to calm down.

When Carol returned, only Kayla's vehicle was in the driveway. Without delay, Carol grabbed her purse and went to knock on the door. However, nobody answered. She banged on the door repeatedly and rang the doorbell, but there was still no answer. It appeared that Kayla had left with her friend.

A sense of defeat swept over Carol. She turned around to head back to her car right as the front door opened.

"I'm sorry. I was in the shower. Can I help you?" Kayla said, wearing only a bath towel.

Carol spun around in shock and said, "I just came over to talk to you for a moment."

"And you are?"

"I'm sorry. My name is Carol. I'm John's wife."

"How dare you come to my house. I don't have anything to say to you." Kayla said as she started to close the door.

"Please give me just one minute of your time."

"Go ahead and say what you have to say then. I need to get back to my shower." Kayla said in a huff.

"It isn't so much anything that I have to say. I wanted to give you something." Carol said as she reached into her purse.

Kayla opened the screen door, and Carol instantly shocks her with a stun gun, dropping Kayla to the ground in agony before forcing herself into the house and dragging Kayla back in. As Kayla laid there trying to regain control of her extremities, Carol zapped her another time. Then she reached into her purse, pulled out some rope, and bound Kayla's hands and feet.

"What the hell are you doing? You're fucking crazy!" Kayla yelled.

"You are a spunky little one, aren't you? We are going to have so much fun together. Well, at least I'm going to enjoy it." Carol told Kayla.

"Bitch, you better let me go or..."

"Or what?" Carol cut her off. "I make the demands, not a homewrecker like you. Now, be a good girl and keep quiet while I get my car. We're going to go on a little trip."

When Carol opened the front door, Kayla yelled at the top of her lungs, "Help! Somebody help me!"

Carol quickly closed the door and said, "I planned over and over how this would go, but I still forgot one thing. Some fucking tape to shut you up!" Carol screeched back at Kayla before hitting her a third time with the stun gun.

With Kayla now disoriented with her surroundings, Carol went outside, opened the garage door, and backed her car into the garage. Noticing the clock on her dashboard, Carol knew time was of utmost importance since the game John was watching would be over soon, and he would probably be on his way to Kayla's place.

When Carol came back into the house, Kayla was regaining clarity.

"Get up!" Carol told Kayla.

"I can't. You have me tied up."

"I told you to get up!" Carol ordered a second time as she pulled Kayla's arms up to help her to her feet.

"Where are you taking me?" Kayla asked.

"Hop down the hallway to the garage."

"You know you're not going to get away with this. John is on his way over here now."

"Hop down the hallway, or you will get shocked again," Carol warned her.

Kayla complied with the order, but only because she feared the stun gun more than where Carol may be taking her. Once they got to the garage, Carol put Kayla into the trunk of her car, retrieved Kayla's phone and house keys, pulled out of the garage, then closed the garage door before driving away.

The rush of pulling off a kidnapping gave Carol a thrill like no other. She felt better than she ever had before. Although she wanted to rush back to her palace and begin Kayla's training, Carol knew she had to be mindful of the laws of the road. It would be most unfortunate for her to get caught now with victory in sight.

Carol made the hour-long journey to her palace without incident and backed her car up to the entrance door.

"Get out of the car," Carol ordered.

Kayla, being the stubborn and non-compliant woman she is, rejected Carol's demands.

"Fine. Have it your way." Carol said as she closed the trunk lid.

Carol went inside and dragged the rope to her car that she had earlier attached to the overhead pulley. When she opened the trunk again, she tied the rope to Kayla's bound hands, went back inside, and pressed the button for the electric motor to drag Kayla's naked body out of the trunk, across the dungeon floor, and hoisted her to her feet.

After closing the doors to her palace, Carol told Kayla, "This all could go so much smoother if you would only learn to listen and obey."

"What the hell is this place? Where am I?" Kayla demanded to know.

As Carol put on her coat due to the air conditioner being set so low, she said, "I'm tired of all of your questions, but since you are new here and, I'm guessing due to your attitude, you will probably be a guest for quite some time, I will allocate some leniency towards you. You are now a guest in my palace and are here for training. From this point forward, you will now refer to me as Lady Carol."

"How does crazy bitch sound? It kind of suits you if you ask me." Kayla responded.

Angered by her defiant remarks, Carol stormed over to her throne and retrieved a metal-studded crop selected specifically for Kayla.

"Address me appropriately or pay the consequences."

"Go to hell!"

Carol swung as hard as she could, and the crop landed with full force across Kayla's left breast. The shock of pain caused Kayla to scream in response louder than Carol had ever heard anyone else in her dungeon.

"Help! Somebody, please get me out of here." Kayla shouted with tears running down her face.

"Help me. Help me." Carol mimicked Kayla. "Scream as much as you want. It's music to my ears. Besides, nobody can hear you anyway. You are in a soundproof building.

"Please let me go. I will do anything you want. Just let me go." Kayla pleaded.

"Oh, I know better than that. I have seen all of the deceitful behavior you exhibit. I've followed you for months and watched you while you were at work. I know the trickery you pull to get what you want. You are far from learning your lesson."

"What do you want?" Kayla asked.

"You can start with respect and address me as Lady Carol!"

"Fine, Lady Carol," Kayla sneered.

"See, that is exactly what I am talking about. You don't have respect for anyone, do you?"

"Respect is earned, not given."

"Then I guess I am just going to have to earn it with five lashes from my whip."

Carol positioned herself behind Kayla and began earning her respect. The first lash landed across her lower back, but Kayla tried her best to muffle her moan to take away the satisfaction Carol received from it. The second lash hit Kayla's side on the tender skin just below her right armpit. That strike caused Kayla to let out a shrill cry.

"Have I earned your respect, or shall I continue?" Carol asked.

"I'm sorry, Lady Carol. I am sorry. Please stop." Kayla sincerely responded between staggered breaths and with tears running down her cheeks.

"That wasn't so hard, was it?"

Kayla could only squeak out a soft "No."

"No what?"

"No, Lady Carol."

"I'll save the rest of your lashes for later. It's probably best to keep you conscious for a while."

"Thank you, Lady Carol. I will do whatever you ask. I promise."

Carol put the handle of the whip under Kayla's chin and said, "What I want is for you to leave my husband alone."

"I will. I promise, Lady Carol."

"The problem is that I don't believe you."

"I won't see him again. I won't call, text, write, or anything else."

"Does my whip need to remind you how to address me?"

"No, Lady Carol."

"I can see why John finds you so attractive. Your skin is beautiful. Nicely tanned, clear complexion, decent bone structure, you are a reasonably attractive woman."

"Thank you, Lady Carol."

Carol retrieved a pot of molten wax from a Bunsen burner near her throne, put it directly under Kayla's face, and asked, "Do you think if you weren't as pretty that John would still love you?"

Kayla looked on in horror and started to squirm around as Carol began making motions as if she would throw the hot wax on her.

Carol put the pot down, grabbed a blindfold, and secured it around Kayla's eyes, saying, "I don't want the wax to ruin your vision. I want you to see how hideous you look every time you pass a mirror. It'll be over with soon. Afterward, I may just let you see my husband, and we can see if he still wants you."

Carol grabbed a glass of ice water sitting on a nearby table and threw it in Kayla's face as she let out another scream anticipating hot wax to scorch her face. Carol laughed so hard at Kayla's reaction that she nearly fell over.

"I am having so much fun with you, but our session needs to pause for a moment. John sent a text to you ten minutes ago asking where you were. Now he sent another text again telling you that he was heading home. I'll come back here in a bit. Until then, I think you should freshen up a bit." Carol said as she turned on the faucet supplying water to the over-head sprinkler. "In case you haven't noticed, it's only sixty degrees in my palace, and the tap water is about fifty degrees. It might get a little chilly for you. Maybe if I turn on the fan to help circulate the air, you would be warmer." Carol giggled.

XVI

〰

Chapter 16

As she left Kayla to freeze, Carol headed home knowing there was still much work to do on Kayla before she would fully submit to Carol's every whim and leave John forever. It was unfortunate that people would start looking for her as soon as John realized she was missing. Time never seems to be on Carol's side.

When Carol arrived at home, she still had about thirty minutes before John would get there, so she whipped up a quick meal for him. It was an unusual gesture on her part since she hadn't done that for him in months, but they needed to talk, and Carol figured the best way to defuse a possible argument was over something like a meal.

"Honey, you're home!" Carol said as soon as John walked in the door.

"Well, I do live here. What's all this?" John asked, pointing to the table set for two.

"I thought we could have a nice meal and talk."

"Not tonight, Carol."

"Why not? Did you have a bad day? Did the Raiders lose?" Carol asked.

"What's going on with you, Carol? Why are you acting so strange?"

"Is it wrong for a wife to desire to talk to her husband?"

"You know what? If you want to talk, I guess there are some things I need to tell you. I was going to wait until next week, but I don't see a reason to postpone it any further." John said as he sat down at the table.

"I've been swamped at work, so the best I could do in a short amount of time was to make spaghetti," Carol said as she placed two prepared plates on the table for them.

"Look, we should just get down to business and talk," John told her.

"Nonsense. We can take a moment to share a meal."

"I'm just going to say it bluntly, Carol. I want a divorce."

"I know. Now let's eat."

"Did you hear what I said?" John asked.

"Yes, honey. I heard you, and I also know about your darling Kayla that you're leaving me for."

"How do you know about her?"

"It doesn't matter. Your plans got mysteriously canceled with her tonight, didn't they? That's why you are in such a bad mood, isn't it?"

"What are you up to, Carol?"

"I just had a little talk with her earlier today. Not much was said, just that she doesn't want to see you any longer."

"Bullshit!" John shouted at Carol.

"No. No, it's the truth. Those words came out of that pretty little mouth of hers. Now eat your dinner before it gets cold. You know, I'm taking some time off work next week. If you can exchange her ticket, I'd love to go to Jamaica with you."

"How did you know about Jamaica?"

"I know everything, John. In my line of work, I have to learn as much as possible about people to ensure a good experience. It turns out that I'm a natural at it." Carol laughed.

John stood up, reached for his phone, and called Kayla.

"I told you she doesn't ever want to speak to you again. She isn't going to answer, honey."

"You know where she is, don't you? Damn it, where is Kayla?" John shouted as he slammed his fist onto the table.

"You sure are upset. Maybe you should go relax in your chair."

"I swear, Carol. If you've done something to her, I will make you pay for it! For the last time, where is she?"

"She's taking a shower and chilling out at my work."

"You better tell me exactly where you work, or I'm going to call the police and tell them you've done something to her."

"What exactly are you going to tell them, John? That your housewife of eighteen years has a secret job that you don't know anything about, including where it's located, and has abducted your mistress that you're engaged to but have no idea where I took her? To me, that sounds a little crazy."

"Maybe I'll just beat it out of you then," John said while taking a threatening stance. "Don't push me, Carol. You have gone too far this time."

"Okay, calm down. I'll take you to her so you can hear it for yourself. But, are you sure you don't want to finish dinner first?"

"Damn it, Carol. I don't want to eat dinner with you. I want to make sure Kayla is okay."

John got into Carol's car, and they made the short drive to Carol's workplace without saying a single word to each other. The drive was just like every other they took together in the past. Stare straight out the window while ignoring each other. Oddly, it somewhat warmed Carol's heart reminiscing about those times they shared.

As Carol pulled into the driveway of her dungeon, John asked, "What is this dump?"

"It's a place I like to call my palace." Carol proudly replied.

After Carol opened the outside door, she told John, "You may be a little angry now, and she's going to break your heart when she tells you that it's over with, but remember that I will always be there for you, John."

"Open the damn door, Carol."

As soon as she opened the door to her palace, a look of horror came across John's face as he saw Kayla strung up naked, with a sprinkler drenching her with water.

John rushed over to Kayla, asking, "Baby, are you okay?"

"Get me out of here, John," Kayla said in a shaky and shivering voice.

"Don't you have anything to say to John?" Carol asked.

"She's fucking crazy."

"I know, baby. Everything will be okay. I'll get you out of here." John told her while already starting to feel the effects of the cold water himself.

As John ripped the power cord of the fan out of the wall and searched for the shutoff valve to the sprinkler, Carol grabbed Kayla by the hair and angrily said, "You told me you would end the relationship and never speak to him again. You lied to me. Do you have any idea how much I hate people lying to me?"

John shut off the sprinkler and returned to Kayla, pushing Carol away from her.

"Kayla, it's almost over. I'll have you out of here in a couple of minutes." John assured her.

However, Carol had other plans. She took out her stun gun and pressed it against his neck, sending him into convulsions on the wet dungeon floor. She then tied him up in a similar fashion as Kayla and used the second overhead pulley to hoist John into the air and to his feet.

"Wow! That was something. Do you know why that zap was so powerful, my dear John? It's the water. Water conducts electricity so much more efficiently. Do you know how I know this?" Carol asked.

John, still dazed from the jolt, could only mumble something unintelligible.

"It is because I have studied, researched, and honed my skills to inflict pain on people. They were all willing participants, so don't worry about that. I didn't think of it as a talent that would pertain to being a life skill. However, it is ironic how those skills came in handy for a time like this."

"Do you think you can get away with this? People will be looking for us." John said with the little bit of energy he could muster.

"Not for at least a week. Besides, all you have to do is promise to leave that whore of yours, and we can walk out of here together."

"I'm not leaving here without Kayla."

"That is a problem, John. I think I'm going to have to work on both of your attitudes."

Carol went back to her throne and instructed Kayla to tell John the appropriate way to address her.

"She wants to be referred to as Lady Carol. If you refuse, she will probably whip you just like she did me, so do what she says.

"Look at that. You're learning quickly, whore. Do what I say. Simple enough of a concept, right John?"

"Screw you. When I get out of these ropes, I'll make sure you get locked up for an exceptionally long time." John told Carol.

"That just got you a few lashes, John. I do not tolerate outbursts, lies, or being disrespected."

Carol grabbed her whip and snapped it across his chest, but she immediately dropped it when she saw the pain it caused him and heard him scream.

Carol walked up to John and whispered into his ear, "I don't want to hurt you, John. I have loved you for a long time. So, every time you fail to obey a command, your little princess over there will suffer for it. Do I make myself clear?"

John looked at Carol with disgust but never said a word. That's when Carol took a few practice swings of the whip in Kayla's direction, inching ever closer to her.

"Okay. I understand." John blurted out.

"You understand what, John?"

"I will obey your commands, Lady Carol." John condescendingly corrected himself.

"Well done, John. There is hope for you yet. However, the

training session for the day is over. I am exhausted. We can start bright and early tomorrow morning."

Carol went out to her car, brought in a handful of clothes and a blanket, and made a makeshift bed next to her throne.

"I do expect the two of you to remain silent while I get my rest. Tomorrow is going to be a long day. If you do disturb me, the sprinkler gets turned back on."

"You don't expect us to stand here all night, do you?"

Carol grabbed the crop off her throne, raced over to Kayla, and gave her three swats across her buttocks. Each of them causing her to scream louder and arch her back further with every swing Carol took.

"You will address me as Lady Carol, John!"

"Damn you, Carol. Hit me and leave Kayla alone. I dare you to hit me! But you are too weak to do that, aren't you?"

"Do not push me, John. You have no idea of what I am capable of doing. Because of that outburst, your princess must be punished."

"It was my fault. Please, leave her alone."

"You are correct, John. It is your fault, and she knows that too. Every outburst you have and every punishment she has to endure is because you don't love her. She will come to see that in time."

Carol grabbed a pair of nipple clamps from a nearby shelf and showed them to John.

"See these clamps. They have sharp little teeth meant to bite into the flesh. I'm going to clamp them down on your whore's nipples and hang weights from them. The pain is quite extreme, and every time she squirms in discomfort, they will slide down bit by bit, cutting into her nipple further. If the clamps are still attached to her by morning, I have ways of making her squirm until they do fall off."

"I beg you, Carol. Please don't do that. I'm the one that you are mad at. Take your anger out on me. I deserve it for what I have done to you. It's all my fault. I take full responsibility for hurting you as I did."

Carol paused for a moment and reflected on the epiphany John just had. She wanted to believe him, but it was probably just a ploy to deflect her attention away from Kayla. Just in case John was honestly stating how he felt and was beginning to realize how much he hurt Carol, she decided to forgo the brutal torture of Kayla for the time being.

"You're fortunate that I won't be putting you through that torment tonight," Carol told Kayla.

"Yes, Lady Carol," Kayla responded.

"Isn't it incredible how a little respect goes a long way? It would be best for you to convince my husband to go along with the program before something terrible does happen to you."

"I agree, Lady Carol," Kayla replied as she glared at John.

"Did you see that look, John? She's getting pissed off at you for the way you treat me. Think about that while I sleep. I'll see you both in the morning."

Carol had a difficult time trying to sleep. It was still chilly in the dungeon, the clothes on the floor didn't make much of a bed, and it was an overall stressful day, but her mind was the biggest culprit. Carol couldn't shut off her mind. It kept racing with different scenarios and outcomes, flashing back to the torment she endured of John's callousness, the affairs that he had, how everything was crumbling around her with little control over anything outside of her decaying palace. Even the power she had within her palace was fading.

Regardless of being sleep-deprived, Carol started her day early as she usually does. She knew it was going to be a day unlike any other as soon as she got up from her makeshift bed since she didn't have a cup of coffee to start it with. Carol sat on her throne and wondered what else would be out of the ordinary before catching a glimpse of John and Kayla once her mind focused on something other than her immediate vicinity.

"Darling, you're awake. You never wake up before me. I hope you slept well."

"You know damn well, Lady Carol, that I didn't sleep a wink being strung up here like a puppet on a string."

"That's a shame, but it pleases me that you remembered my proper name."

"You have made it quite memorable for me, Lady Carol."

"What about you whore? Did you find your accommodations satisfactory?" Carol asked Kayla.

"Yes, Lady Carol."

"Wow. Two for two. You both must have had a lot of time to think last night. That's good. I had a lot of time last night to contemplate our little situation as well."

"Lady Carol, can I have a word with you in private?" John asked.

"No. Anything you have to say, you can say in front of your whore. There are no longer any secrets between the three of us."

"I know I've been a horrible husband to you. I took everything you did for me for granted. I had many affairs that broke your heart multiple times, yet you kept trying to be a perfect wife to me. I love you for that. I love you for who you are, Carol. I love you."

"That is so sweet, John, but you don't find me attractive. You said it yourself many times."

"I was an ass. You are the most beautiful woman I have ever known, inside and out."

"Are you willing to prove that to me?" Carol asked.

"If you let me down, I will make love to you right here in front of her to prove it to both of you."

"As tempting as that is, I had something else in mind."

"Anything, Carol. Just name it, and I will prove to you that you are the only woman I desire."

"I will let you down if you give her twenty lashes with the whip while telling her how hideous she is to you."

"I would, but I've lost sensation in my arms and hands. I can't hold a pencil, let alone brandish a whip."

"That's okay, John. I'll give you time to recover."

"Then, yes. I'll do it."

Kayla pleaded with John, "Please don't do this. I love you."

"Shut up, whore!" Carol screamed as she slapped Kayla across the face.

"Once I do this, we can leave and start our life anew, right?" John asked.

"We? As in all of us?" Carol asked in response.

"No. You and me. Just the two of us."

"John! Don't do this to me." Kayla cried out.

Carol retrieved the control box for the overhead pulley to lower John down, but she had one question to ask him before she pressed the button.

"Do you think I'm stupid, John?"

"What? Why would you think that?"

"Because I know you're going to try to overpower me once you regain use of your hands. You have no intention of hurting her even remotely close to as much as you have hurt me."

"That's not true. I love you, Carol."

"Oh, how I wish that were the truth."

"It is the truth! You can believe me. I'm never going to lie to you again."

"I don't know what to believe. I can no longer tell the difference between what's real and what isn't. I thought I could be the perfect wife to you so you would love me forever, but I was delusional because I knew deep down that I would never be enough for you. I created the appearance of an ideal home and marriage to the outside world, but it was a deception perpetrated by me to hide my embarrassment. Then, I created my palace. This dump that you're standing in right now. This was the world that I made where I had control, where I was desired and worshipped, where I had strength and power. However, this was also just a fantasy. My entire life has been nothing but a series of illusions I invented to hide from reality, but that ends now." Carol said as she retrieved a pistol kept under her throne.

"Carol, you don't have to do this," John said in his typical salesman voice, trying to convince Carol to stop.

"I do, John. There isn't any other way to end this madness. However, I do have a dilemma. If I kill Kayla, you'll find a replacement for her, and this will continue carrying on forever because it is who you are. Yet, if I shoot you, I lose the man that I have gone to great lengths to fight for. The only man that I have loved and gave myself wholly to. Decisions, decisions." Carol said as she outstretched her arms and twirled around.

The world spun around Carol in a dizzying mix of emotions. She began to feel like she was in a vortex that pulled her deeper into the darkness of hate and anger. Carol suddenly stopped spinning around when the solution to her problems popped into her head.

"I give up. I realize that there isn't a way for me to win this war. So I surrender, but I do so on my terms. I hope the two of you will be happy till death do you part." Carol told them as she raised the gun, bent her elbow, pressed it to her head, and pulled the trigger.

Carol's lifeless body fell to the ground in a pool of blood at John and Kayla's feet leaving them to fulfill their destiny of being together for as long as that may be.

Epilogue

Suicide and/or violence is never the solution to any problem. If you or someone you know are having these thoughts, immediately call the national suicide hotline, a therapist, or local law enforcement for immediate assistance.

Acknowledgement

I owe a great deal of gratitude to Dusty S. for her time, energy, and input. Your help was instrumental for me to find the time to finish this book. Without you, this novel would still be nothing more than an unused file on my computer.

I would also like to thank Lisa E., Suzi P., Lisa W., Karen D., and Deedra L. for their time reading my manuscript and their feedback. Your insight is appreciated more than I can say.

Finally, I want to thank my longtime friends Tracey C., Lisa W., and Kay S. for believing in my abilities and encouraging me to write.

About The Author

Brian Romesburg & Jack

Who Is Brian Scott Romesburg?

I am originally from California and have extensively traveled the country before settling down in Indiana with my dog, Jack. Although I have written many stories, I've only shared them with close friends until now. With their encouragement, I am proud to share my premier novel Illusions of Reality with you and the world!

Learn more about me, be part of crafting my next novel, send me an email, and have discussions on my forum at

www.BrianScottRomesburg.com